'I seduced yo

Was it any wond
one another? She
whole body shaking
shattered by that one starkly cruel statement. She ran from the room, her one thought to get away from this nightmare. Wrenching the front door open, she raced down the drive then stood panting at the bottom with tears rolling down her face as she tried to decide where to go next.

Dear Reader

With the long summer evenings, what better way to relax than by reading a selection of stories which really take you away from it all? With four exciting contemporary romances, Mills & Boon will transport you to some of the most exotic locations in the world. Enjoy the luxury of those places you always wanted to visit...surely the perfect chance to dream of your ideal man! Look out for our summer packs in your local shops or contact our Reader Service and indulge yourself in the world of romance!

The Editor

Jennifer Taylor was born in Liverpool, England, and still lives in the north-west, several miles outside the city. Books have always been a passion of hers, so it seemed natural to choose a career in librarianship, a wise decision as the library is where she met her husband, Bill. Twenty years and two children later they are still happily married and she is still working in the library, with the added bonus that she has discovered how challenging and enjoyable writing romantic fiction can be!

Recent titles by the same author:

OLD LOVE, NEW LOVE

PROMISE ME LOVE

BY

JENNIFER TAYLOR

MILLS & BOON LIMITED
ETON HOUSE, 18-24 PARADISE ROAD
RICHMOND, SURREY TW9 1SR

First published in Great Britain 1993
by Mills & Boon Limited

This edition 1993

ISBN 0 263 78084 8

Set in Times Roman 11 on 12 pt.
01-9307-50263 C

Made and printed in Great Britain

CHAPTER ONE

HE WAS late.

Beth picked up the glass of mineral water, her hand shaking so that it clinked against her teeth as she sipped. She set it down again then clasped her hands tightly together as she fought down the growing sense of panic. She'd known all along that he'd been reluctant when she'd arranged this meeting, but he would come... he must!

The restaurant door opened and she swung round, hope flaring in her soft hazel eyes, but it wasn't him. Where was he? Why was he so late? Surely he wouldn't stand her up after promising to meet her? The fear grew until she felt sick and she swallowed hard.

'If you're waiting for Andrew then I'm afraid you're in for a disappointment, because he isn't coming, not now, not ever!'

The woman's voice was shrill and Beth jumped, her head turning in shock. She'd been so engrossed in her own thoughts that she'd not noticed the woman stopping by her table and now she stared at her in surprise.

'I'm sorry. Were you speaking to me?'

'Who else?' The woman glared at her, her face filled with contempt. 'Women like you make me sick! You don't give a damn who you hurt, do you, as long as you get what you want?' She slammed her hand on the table, making the glass tilt so that water spilled on to the pale pink cloth. 'Well, now it's over, do you hear me? Over! You stay away from Andrew from now on or you'll regret it!'

'I . . .' Beth stared at her in confusion as the fear blossomed until it filled every scrap of her being. What was going on? Who was this woman? And why did she think that she had the right to warn her to stay away from Andrew?

She drew in a shaky breath, only barely aware that people were watching them. It didn't seem to matter about other people right then; nothing mattered apart from finding out what was going on. 'Who are you? What do you want?'

Her voice shook and the other woman smiled tightly, a faint triumph on her face. 'Who do you think I am? I'm Andrew's wife, of course. Don't try pretending that you didn't know he was married because it won't work. That was probably part of his attraction for you!'

'Married?' Beth repeated the words, her lips barely moving, her face waxen as all the colour drained away.

'Yes, married. Oh, don't come the innocent with me now. You knew all along, the same as you knew about the children, but you didn't let either fact stop you from chasing him. He's told me all about it, the way you pursued him relentlessly even though he kept on telling you that he wasn't interested. But you wouldn't take no for an answer, would you? You kept on until you wore down his resistance. I don't blame him as much as I blame you. You're nothing but a little who——!'

'Is everything all right, darling? I don't know exactly what is going on here, but you two ladies seem to be attracting a great deal of attention.'

The voice was gently amused and Beth swung round to stare at the tall man standing behind her chair. Just for a moment her eyes met the cool grey ones which were watching her intently before she looked away as the shock hit her afresh. Andrew was married, had children, had lied about everything!

She swayed in the seat and would have fallen if hands hadn't fastened around her shoulders to hold her steady. This time when the man spoke there was no amusement in his voice, just a cold hauteur which made Andrew's wife step uncertainly away from the table.

'I still don't know exactly what's going on here, but I don't think this is either the time or the place for this sort of discussion.' He stared at the woman, his face set into grim lines. 'We had been intending to lunch here, but in the circumstances that is out of the question now.'

'Lunch . . . you . . . her? But I thought . . . I thought . . .' She looked from the man to Beth, her eyes stopping on his hands, which were still resting on Beth's shoulders, and her face crumpled. 'You mean that you didn't come here to meet Andrew?'

Beth tried to speak, tried her hardest to force an answer out from lips which felt cold and stiff, but it was impossible. Was this what dying felt like, this numbness, this coldness in the soul? It had taken all her courage to arrange this meeting, to ring Andrew and force him to agree to see her, and now she had none left.

She shuddered, her whole body trembling, and the hands tightened so that the man's fingers bit into her flesh in a way that was oddly comforting.

'We came here to have lunch. Does that answer your question?' There was a cold dismissal in the deep voice now and the woman gave an anguished little moan before pushing past him and running from the restaurant.

'Come along. Let's get you out of here.' The man slid a hand under her elbow and half lifted her to her feet, then guided her through the maze of tables towards the door. Beth could feel the curious stares they were attracting, hear the faint whispers, but it felt as though it were all happening to someone else. Deep down she knew she had to shake herself out of this trance, but it seemed beyond her capabilities at this moment. Her whole world seemed to have shrunk to a few brief words and one stark fact: Andrew was married!

Dropping some money on to the cashier's desk, the man opened the door and steered her outside, steadying her as she stumbled over the step. 'Just take your time. My car's over there. Can you walk that far or do you want me to carry you?'

Beth shook her head, her face the colour of putty, her eyes filled with despair. 'No, you've done enough. I . . . I'll be all right now.'

She tried to ease her arm away, but his fingers merely fastened tighter around it. 'You're not all right. So don't act stupid. If I let go of you you'll end up in the gutter from the look of you. Just do as you're told and stop being more of a fool than it appears you've been already.'

That stung and her head came up as she glared at him. 'I never asked for your help or your opinions, thank you.'

'Nobody said that you did, but you're getting both for free. Now unless you want to continue making a spectacle of yourself for the enjoyment of everyone back there then I suggest that you get into the car.' He nodded towards the restaurant and Beth felt her cheeks burn when she saw the interested faces watching them through the window. She let him lead her to the car and climbed inside without another word, sitting stiffly in the soft leather seat while he slid behind the wheel.

'Fasten your seatbelt.' He shot her a quick glance as he started the engine, waiting patiently while she struggled to snap the buckle into place with trembling fingers.

'Here, let me do it.' He pushed her hands aside and dealt with the belt, leaning sideways so that his hair brushed her cheek. It smelled clean and fresh, just like Andrew's hair always did, and Beth felt tears sting her eyes. She turned her head to stare out of the side window, wondering what she was going to do now, how she would manage. She was twenty-two years old and her life was in tatters. There was no one to turn to, no one to offer help or comfort. She was completely on her own from here on in.

'There's no point in crying. It won't help. All it will do is make you feel rotten.'

She jumped when the man spoke, turning to glance at him as she rubbed a hand over her wet face. In the light spilling through the windscreen his face looked stern and remote, his grey eyes cool, his thick blond hair more silver than gold. He was a stranger, so what was she doing getting in the car with him like this?

Panic rose in a sudden, sharp surge and he must have seen and understood the reason for it because he smiled tightly as he skimmed a long, cool look over her.

'You can stop worrying about my intentions. You are quite safe. I don't kick a person when he or, in this case, she is down. Just tell me where you live and I'll drive you home. And, as I said before, forget about the tears because they won't help a bit.'

Why did she believe him? For a moment Beth struggled to reason it out, but couldn't; yet she knew instinctively that he meant her no harm. She fumbled in her bag for a tissue and wiped her face. He was right, of course. No amount of tears would change the fact that Andrew had lied to her. It was something she was going to have to come to terms with. She had loved him so much and he had taken every scrap of that love and used it to his own ends.

'That's better. Now if you'll just give me the directions then I'll soon have you home.' He slid the car into gear, but Beth hurriedly shook her head.

'No. I can't go home just yet. My flatmate is entertaining her boyfriend and I told her I would be out until the evening. If you can just take me to...' she hesitated, wondering where exactly to tell him, then chose the first place that came into her head '...the river.'

He shook his head as he eased the car into the flow of traffic, his mouth an uncompromising line. 'No way. What kind of a fool do you take me for?'

'I don't know what you mean.'

'Don't you? Then let me spell it out for you: there is no way that I am taking you to the river in your state of mind. Understand?'

'My state of...' Her face burned with angry colour. 'I might be upset, but I'm not suicidal! Don't be ridiculous. Do I look like that sort of a person?'

'You look like a woman who has just been kicked in the teeth and I know from bitter experience that that can put the craziest thoughts into the sanest person's head. There is no way I am going to have you on my conscience if you do anything stupid, so the river is out. Think of somewhere else.' He swung the car down a side-street, slowing as he came to a junction, and Beth gripped hold of her bag as she fumbled for the door-handle.

'I'm getting out. I've had enough today to last me a lifetime and I don't need you hurling insults to complete the picture!' She tugged on the latch, but the door refused to open despite her efforts.

'Save your strength. It's on a central-locking system. It won't open until I release it and I have no intention of doing that just yet.' He took advantage of a gap in the traffic to cross the junction, picking up speed as the road cleared.

Beth sat back and closed her eyes in despair. It was all too much to deal with, this virtual abduction coming on top of the shock of Andrew's deceit. She just didn't have the strength to argue any more.

'Have you thought of some place else you'd like to go?' The man's voice was softer now, the deep tones less abrasive, and she felt a ridiculous lump come into her throat. She swallowed hard and shook her head, keeping her face averted. He swore softly and pulled the car into the kerb, then stopped the engine. Beth could feel him watching her, but she refused to look at him, refused to allow another human being to witness the naked despair which must be etched in her eyes.

'What's your name?'

She swallowed against the choking lump, her voice muffled when she finally answered. 'Beth.'

'Well, Beth, I know this must feel like the end of the world for you right now, but you will get over it in time. It hurts like hell, I know, but the pain will become tolerable after a while.'

She shook her head. 'It won't. It isn't that simple.'

'It is.' He took her hands in his, smoothing her cold fingers in a way that was oddly comforting. 'You're better off without this guy...what was his name?'

'Andrew.' It hurt even to whisper the name, to remember all the other times she'd said it in joy, in love, and a tiny dry sob escaped her lips.

His fingers tightened around hers, warm and hard, but they couldn't melt the ice that was flowing through her and after another moment he let her go. 'Look, Beth, I don't know the full story, but it was obvious from what little I heard that Andrew has been spinning you a line and that you had no idea he was married.'

'No, none at all. I would never have gone out with him if I'd known.' It seemed strangely important that he believe her and she opened her eyes at last to look at him. 'You do believe me, don't you?'

He nodded. 'Yes, of course I do. I would have needed to be blind not to see the shock on your face when that woman told you who she was. But can't you see that you've had a lucky escape? I know you're hurt and upset and that it must feel as though the world has ended, but it's better to find out the truth in the end than go on living a lie.'

'I...' She looked away, staring at the traffic as it drove past where they were parked. So many people going on their way, their lives undisturbed, while here she sat with her life in tatters. It wasn't fair!

'I know you won't believe me, Beth, but in a year or so's time you will look back on this and probably laugh about it, most likely won't be able to remember what he looks like.'

He meant what he said to offer comfort, but it didn't do that. It only intensified the futility of it all. How could she ever forget Andrew now? How?

'No.' Her voice was so low that he had to lean sideways to hear it. 'I won't forget. I can't!'

'You will, Beth. It will take time and it will be painful, but in the end you will put this behind you and——'

'I'm pregnant.' She stared back at him, her face white, her eyes dark with despair. 'I won't be able to forget Andrew because I'm carrying his child. Now do you understand?'

Shock and a fleeting, bitter pain flashed unexpectedly in his eyes before abruptly he turned away, his hands tightening on the steering-wheel as he muttered, 'Dear God... not again!'

It seemed a strange thing for him to say, but Beth didn't dwell on it as the full impact of what had happened hit her afresh. A shudder ran through her and she clenched her hands as she strove to hold on to her control. She was alone and pregnant and somehow she had to find a way to cope with it. Somehow she had to find the strength to rebuild her shattered life not only for herself but for the coming child.

The coffee was cold. Beth set the cup down carefully on the table and stared blankly round the room. It had been a mistake coming here. She should have insisted that he let her out of the car before, but instead she had let him bring her back to his flat and make her coffee that she didn't want.

'Sorry about that. Business. It's impossible to escape even at home some days.'

He came back from answering the phone and Beth glanced round, searching his face for any signs of the regret he must surely feel at being landed with her like this. However there was nothing but a faint concern in those cool grey eyes as he noticed the untouched cup of coffee.

'Let me make you some fresh. That's gone cold.' He reached for the cup, but Beth snatched it back, flushing as her fingers brushed against his in her haste. She shook her head, feeling the pale red-gold hair spilling from its knot on top of her head to fall around her face. She must look a sight with her tear-streaked face and tangled hair and she wished harder than ever that she'd insisted he let her out of the car when she'd had the chance. She didn't want his kindness or his pity. Neither would help! 'I don't want any more, thank you. I've already disrupted your day quite enough. I expect this is the last time you'll play the Good Samaritan. You certainly got more than you bargained for today, didn't you?'

She forced a shaky smile, seeing the way his eyes narrowed thoughtfully on her before he gave a thin smile of his own as he sat down opposite her at the table. 'I must admit none of this was on the agenda.' He held up one large, beautifully shaped hand and ticked an imaginary list off his fingers. 'Breakfast meeting with clients, a spot of paperwork, stock-check at the factory, then an early lunch followed by much the same as the morning's schedule. You're quite right, nowhere on the list do I recall anything about helping a lady in distress!'

He was quietly teasing her to make her feel more at ease, but it only made her feel worse when she realised how she must have messed up his busy day. 'I'm sorry,' she repeated.

'What for?' He reached for the pot and poured himself some coffee, grimacing as he took a sip of the cold liquid. 'That's revolting. Are you sure I can't make you some fresh?'

'No, really. I don't want anything. And I meant that I was sorry for ruining your day when it's obvious that you are a very busy man.'

He shrugged as he pushed the cup aside. 'Not so busy that I can't spare time to help someone who obviously needed it.'

'Why did you help me?' She twisted the cup round on its saucer, then stopped when coffee spilled over the side. 'Most people would have run a mile from the confrontation I was having, so what made you decide to help?'

She glanced up at him curiously, then felt a shiver run through her as she caught the fleeting expression of sadness which crossed his face. He seemed to collect himself all of a sudden, his face smoothing into its customary lines which betrayed little of what he was thinking.

'Just an impulse. You looked so shocked that I reacted without thinking about it. I had the feeling that you were about to keel over at any moment.'

'I nearly did. I never... Andrew never...' She took a slow, painful breath. 'I never suspected that he was married. I feel such a fool now and so...well, so guilty!'

'Why? You weren't to know. He went to great lengths to stop you from finding out, presumably. You aren't guilty of anything, Beth.'

'No? I'm pregnant. That's hardly something to celebrate in the circumstances!'

'Yes, you're pregnant, but why? Because you fell in love and this child is the result of that love. You can't blame yourself for that.'

'Maybe not, but I should have been more careful. I did try taking the Pill, but it made me feel so sick, and Andrew said that he would take care of...' She broke off abruptly, staring down at the pool of coffee in the saucer, wondering why she was telling him such things.

He swore softly, his hand closing over hers for a moment before he let it go just as abruptly. 'Men like Andrew should be made to take the consequences for their actions, but they always get away with it one way or another. What are you going to do now? Are you going to have the baby, Beth?'

She looked up with shock in her eyes. 'Of course! I couldn't get rid of it. I couldn't live with myself if I did that.'

'Then how are you going to manage? I assume Andrew knows nothing about the child, so are you going to try and contact him again?'

'No!' She shook her head then smoothed the silky strands of hair back from her face. Her hair was very fine, curling and waving past her shoulders in baby-soft tendrils. She always wore it drawn into a knot and now that it was loose it seemed to move and float with every slight turn of her head. 'I only found out about the baby two days ago myself—found out for definite, that is. I'd had my suspicions for a couple of weeks, but I said nothing to Andrew. Not that he's been around much recently.' She smiled bitterly. 'It took me all my time to make him agree to meet me today, but I should have known better than to...' She broke off, swallowing hard against the lump of pain. 'I was going to tell him today, but there's no point now. It will achieve nothing, only cause more upset to his wife and family, and that's the last thing I want to do!'

'But he should be made to pay towards the child's support. Think this through sensibly, Beth, before you make any decisions you could come to regret. Babies are expensive. You are going to need every penny you can get to support this child.'

'You sound as though you speak from experience.' She gave a brittle little laugh which held scant humour. He was right, but there was no way she was going begging to Andrew for a penny after what he'd done. She would take care of the child herself...she would!

'Some... A...friend of mine found herself in much the same position as you, and I know how hard she struggled to make ends meet at times.'

There it was again, that fleeting hint of some bitter memory, but Beth had her own problems without going into his. 'I don't intend to ask him for a penny! I shall manage. I have a good job and somewhere to live. Hundreds of women have less than me and manage to survive.'

'You have no friends or family who can help you?'

'No. My mother died a few years ago and there's no one else, no sisters or brothers. As for friends...' She shrugged. 'I haven't lived in London long, just over a year, in fact. The friends I've made aren't close enough to turn to now.' She gave a sad little laugh. 'I didn't really seem to need any close friends once I'd met Andrew, if you want the truth. And as for the ones I left behind when I moved, well, they have their own lives, their own problems; I can't suddenly turn up on their doorsteps and burden them with mine. I shall cope.'

'It is your right to claim child support, Beth. You can't afford to worry about Andrew's family when it's blatantly obvious that he didn't give a damn about them himself.' His voice was deep and assured and she glanced at him in surprise.

'You sound like a lawyer. Are you?'

He shook his head. 'Not any longer. Oh, I trained in law and practised for a number of years, but I gave it up. However, I remember enough to state that you are entitled to maintenance for the child.'

'Well, I don't want it!' She pushed back the chair and stood up. 'I've already told you that I don't want anything from Andrew. The baby is mine and as far as I am concerned he has nothing to do with it any longer. He gave up any rights he had when he told that first lie!'

The man stood up also, towering over her in the close confines of the room. 'Then all I can do is wish you luck. It won't be easy but I'm sure you will manage. You have guts, Beth, I can see that. You'll make it.'

He held his hand out and Beth slid her fingers into his, feeling the shiver which rippled along her skin with a start of surprise. Just for a moment she let her eyes linger on the clean, almost angular lines of his face, the steadfastness of his grey eyes, and felt a tiny ache of regret throb in her heart. If she'd had to go and fall in love why couldn't it have been with someone like him? He would never have let her down, would never have lied to her, used her, then cast her aside.

'Thank you,' she said quietly. 'You've been very kind, Mr...' She stopped and smiled wryly. 'I've just realised that I don't know your name.'

He laughed deeply. 'I guess we never had time to get around to that. It's Kane, David Kane.'

Beth returned the pressure of his fingers, then removed her hand and picked up her bag. 'Then thank you again, David Kane.'

She left the room, walking swiftly along the hall to the front door to open it.

'Would you like me to drive you home?'

He had followed to stand just behind her, so close that she brushed against him as she turned. She stepped back a pace, aware that her control had reached its limit. Now all she wanted was to be by herself, to make plans, to just have time to absorb everything that had happened. 'No, thank you. I prefer to be alone so that I can think everything through.'

'Then I want you to promise me something.' In the shadowy hallway his face was grave, his eyes shadowed, and for some strange reason Beth found herself unable to look away from the hypnotic gaze.

'What?'

'That you will come to me if you ever need help.'

'I...' She nodded quickly, strangely touched by the request. 'I promise.'

'Good.' Very gently he smoothed a wispy curl behind her ear, his fingers lingering for a moment longer than was strictly necessary, before his hand fell to his side.

Beth turned and ran down the steps, fighting the almost overwhelming urge to turn back and ask him there and then for help. She couldn't do that. David Kane had helped her enough today, doing more than most people would ever have done, and she didn't have the right to ask him for anything else. Now it was up to her to work things out, to cast aside all the foolish dreams and face up to reality.

CHAPTER TWO

SHE shouldn't have come. All the time the bus was making its way across town Beth had tried to convince herself that she was doing the right thing, but now that she was here she knew it had been a mistake. An act of kindness and a hastily given promise made nearly a month ago didn't constitute an obligation on either side.

She turned to go, then stopped when the front door of the block of flats opened and a tall blond-haired man came out. He didn't notice her standing in the shadows of the trees which lined the drive and Beth shrank back, praying that he wouldn't. As she watched, a woman followed him out of the door, laughing as she linked her arm through his, and stood on tiptoe to whisper something in his ear. He laughed deeply, bending to drop a light kiss on her parted red lips before turning to lead her over to where his car was parked. And that was when he suddenly caught sight of Beth.

'Beth! What are you doing here?'

There was no mistaking the surprise in his voice and Beth felt hot colour glow in her cheeks. It was obvious that he had never expected to see her again, so how was she going to extricate herself from this situation without embarrassing them both?

'Hello, David. I was just passing and thought I'd call in on the off-chance that you were at home, but I can see that you're on your way out so I won't delay you.'

She gave him a brief, tight smile, then started back down the drive. It had seemed like her one last ray of hope, but now she could see how foolish it had been to come here and expect a stranger to solve her problems for her.

'Wait!' He came after her and caught her arm to swing her round. 'What's happened? You must have had a reason for coming, so tell me what it was, Beth.'

She shook her head, looking away from the intent stare. She'd been a fool to come, but she wouldn't make herself an even bigger one by explaining why she had. How *could* she explain that it had been the memory of his kindness that day that had kept her going these past weeks as one problem after another presented itself?

'Come on. Something has happened, hasn't it, Beth?' His voice was low, filled with such concern that she had to physically stop herself from pouring out the whole tale there and then.

'No. Really. I... I shouldn't have come.'

'David... darling! Come on. We're going to be late!' There was undisguised impatience in the woman's voice and Beth looked past him with an apologetic grimace.

'I seem to be holding you up. I'm sorry.'

He cast a fleeting glance over his shoulder, arrogance in the tilt of his head. 'Never mind about Janette. There is no way that you're leaving here without telling me what's wrong.'

Suddenly, irrationally, his attitude annoyed her, and Beth pulled her arm free. 'I've already told you!

It was just an impulse that made me call round, but now I've changed my mind. Don't let me delay you any longer. It might not worry you that your friend is annoyed at having her evening spoiled, but it worries me that I am the cause of it!'

His mouth thinned as he stared coldly back at her. 'I don't want to spoil anyone's evening, but let's get this into perspective, shall we? Janette and I were going to the opera, a very pleasant and enjoyable way to spend a few hours, granted, but hardly a matter of urgency. It is immaterial whether we go tonight, tomorrow, or any damned night this week! It occurred to me that whatever had brought you here must be far more urgent, but if you prefer not to tell me then have it your own way. I'll be seeing you, Beth . . . maybe.'

He turned to walk back to the car and Beth chewed her lip as she watched him go. If she left now then she could never come back again and she desperately needed to talk to someone.

'David, I . . .' She drew in a determined breath, fighting against the despair which had been her companion these past few days. 'I need to talk to someone. That's why I came.'

He stopped at once, his eyes like quicksilver as they skimmed over her strained face before he felt in the pocket of his dinner-jacket and handed her a key. 'Let yourself into the flat. Remember which one it is . . . number twenty-two, second floor on the left? I shall have to make some arrangements for Janette, but I'll be back as soon as I can. Wait for me, Beth.'

Beth nodded obediently as she took the key. She avoided Janette's hostile stare as she hurried into the building and let herself into the flat, then made her way to the kitchen. For long minutes she stood in the doorway remembering the last time she'd been there, when the pain of Andrew's deception had been so sharp and fresh. Now it had faded to a dull, ever-present throb, superseded by events that had happened since. A few weeks ago she'd thought in her naïveté that she'd hit rock-bottom; now she knew that had only been a taster of what was to come. Reality was colder and starker than she'd imagined.

There was a sudden knock at the door and she hurried to answer it, surprised to find David standing outside so soon.

'You found the flat all right, I see. Have you made yourself a drink?' He walked past her, pulling his bow-tie undone as he closed the door firmly behind him.

'No, I haven't had a chance to even think about it. You were so quick.'

'Janette decided she would prefer to take a taxi and I was lucky enough to stop one at the end of the road.' He led the way into the sitting-room and picked up a bottle to pour himself a small measure of whisky. 'Want one?'

'No, thank you. Look, David, I didn't mean to make things difficult for you. Was Janette very annoyed about me turning up and spoiling your evening? Is that why she took a taxi?'

He shrugged carelessly, dropping down into one of the huge leather armchairs and crossing his long legs as he took a swallow of the drink, then closed his eyes. 'Probably. But it was her decision.' He opened his eyes and looked directly at Beth over the rim of the glass. 'Don't start worrying again. Janette and I are old friends—more than mere friends, if you want the truth, but we are both free to do what we choose. If I've had to make alterations to our plans then it's unfortunate, but she is well aware of the rules. What I decide to do and why is my business. Understand?'

Beth nodded, unease rippling down her spine. She'd clung to the memory of his kindness like a talisman, but now he sounded so cold and hard that she didn't know what to think any longer. Heaven knew she was no judge of men if her disastrous affair with Andrew was a yardstick to measure by, but had she been mistaken about David Kane as well?

She walked over to the window and stared out across the tree-tops, her hands twisting the soft folds of her grey coat. Autumn was just setting in, turning the leaves gold and russet. By spring the baby would be born, but she still had to get through all the long dark days first. Was she being foolish to imagine that talking to David Kane could help her do that?

'Want to tell me about it, Beth?' His voice was soft and quiet and she turned slowly to look at him.

Just for a moment she hesitated, then went and sat down in the chair opposite his. 'I don't know where to start.'

'Try taking it from the beginning. It sounds trite, but it's usually the best place.'

'I...' She closed her eyes as she tried to get it all into some sort of sequence, yet the words still rushed out, betraying her fear. 'I've lost my job and I'm going to lose my home and, frankly, I don't know what to do next!'

'I see.' He took another swallow of the whisky, his face betraying nothing. What was he thinking? Was he regretting his previous kindness; was he now sorry that he had become involved in her affair? It was impossible to tell what was going on inside his head. Life had taught David Kane to hide his feelings and he did it well, so well that Beth suddenly regretted coming up to his flat.

She jumped to her feet, colour flaring in her cheeks. 'This has been a mistake. You don't want to hear my problems.'

'Sit down.' He didn't raise his voice, yet she found herself obeying. She sat down abruptly, shaken by the easy authority he displayed, the total conviction that an order given would be obeyed. Who was this man called David Kane? The warm, kind, caring man who had offered comfort to a stranger, or a cold, ruthless dictator who seemingly cut his own path through life?

'How did you lose your job? You were confident that you would be able to support yourself on what you earned so it seems unlikely that you would do anything to jeopardise it.'

'I didn't.' She smiled bitterly. 'Well, that's not quite true. I got pregnant.'

'That's hardly a reason to sack you. There are laws to protect women from that, Beth.'

'I know, I know. I've become an expert on them in the last few weeks! However, it appears that they don't apply in my case. I've been with this firm a little over four months, still on a trial basis, in fact. I'd been with the other company for three years, transferring from the Liverpool branch to the London one. I would have been entitled to full maternity benefits if I'd still been with them, but now...' She broke off and took a deep breath to ease the constriction brought on by anxiety. 'Andrew had been pressing me to go on holiday, but there was no way I could afford it on the salary I earned then. When this job was advertised—secretary to the assistant manager—I jumped at it even though it meant leaving a firm I'd been so happy with. It would have been fine if I hadn't got pregnant.'

'Did they actually dismiss you because of that? That is against the law no matter how long you've been there.'

She shook her head so that a silky curl slid from the pins. 'Oh, no. They weren't that stupid. I was dismissed for bad timekeeping. I've been sick a lot of mornings and had an official warning about three weeks ago. Then when it happened again last week that was that.'

'But surely you explained why?' His face darkened in anger.

'Of course, and that probably put the final nail in the coffin! I think they half suspected anyway. They were very careful about how they put it, but the end result was that I was out. Oh, I'm not stupid, David. I've been to the Citizens' Advice Bureau and the DSS, but neither of them think that I'd have a case if I took the firm to a tribunal, and what's the point in doing that? It wouldn't change the fact that I'm out of work. I've put my name down with a few office temping agencies and done an odd day or two, but the fact that my references are hardly glowing and I was dismissed doesn't endear me to them, and that's even allowing for the fact that they don't as yet know that I am pregnant.' She pressed her hand protectively against the still flat plane of her stomach, her face wistful. 'I'm barely three months pregnant, but what happens in a few months' time when I'm five or six months and as big as a house? I can't see any of the agencies sending me out in that state, can you?'

'I see. You really do seem to have a problem. Have you thought any more about contacting the child's father? Surely in the circumstances he would be prepared to help you?'

'Even if he were, which I doubt, I wouldn't ask him! I don't want anything from him, not a single penny!'

'Don't you think that's foolish?'

'It would be far more foolish to go begging to him! It would achieve nothing, only hurt his wife and children, and that is something I won't have on my conscience. I don't want him to ever find out about this child; he doesn't deserve to.'

'So, in reality, he gets off scot-free while you struggle and worry. You must still care for him, Beth, if you want to protect him, despite what you say.' He swirled the whisky around the glass, yet she had the feeling that he wasn't really seeing it. What was he thinking about? What hurt was he remembering that showed so fleetingly on his face? However, before she could make up her mind whether she should ask him or not, he looked up again, once more in control. 'You mentioned something about losing your home; is that because you can no longer afford to live there?'

'Not immediately, although it would become a problem soon, the way my savings are draining away now that I'm not earning a proper salary. The girl I share the flat with actually owns it. I just rent a room from her and now that she's getting married she has given me notice to leave. I have until the end of the month to find somewhere else, although heaven knows where that will be. Flats are impossible to come by without decent employment references, not to mention a hefty deposit.'

'Then what do you intend to do?'

She shrugged, brushing impatiently at the wisps of hair which tickled her cheek. In the dim light spilling through the window her hair gleamed like burnished gold, a stark contrast to her pale skin. 'I've been trying to work it all out . . . what to do, where to go, but I keep going round in circles. That's why I came tonight to see you.'

'You want me to help you?' There was a cynically hard note in his voice and she flinched, then felt the colour flood her face as she realised what interpretation he had put on her actions in coming here and telling him the whole sorry tale! She jumped to her feet, glaring down at him, hating him for imagining that.

'I didn't come here to ask you for money! I came because you were the only person I could think of who might spare the time to listen to my problems and maybe offer a few words of advice, but obviously I was mistaken!'

'And obviously I was mistaken too. Sit down, Beth. Stop making a scene.'

'I don't want to sit down. I'm leaving before you accuse me of anything else!'

'And where do you intend to go? Back to the flat you are going to have to vacate in a few weeks' time? Hurt pride is a luxury you can ill afford at present.'

'Pride is the only thing I have left!'

Anger shone in her hazel eyes and she heard him sigh roughly. He set the glass down with a thud, then stood up and walked over to the window. 'Pride won't pay the bills, Beth, nor will it put a roof over your head.'

The words were blunt, but to Beth's sensitive ears they sounded as though they held the faintest hint of an apology, and that more than anything stopped her from walking out as she'd intended. She stared at his broad back, feeling the heat of her anger fading. Was it any wonder that he had imagined the worst, after all? They were strangers, nothing more, nothing less. The realisation was suddenly strangely depressing.

'I didn't come here to ask you for money, David. Please believe that.'

He turned to face her, stern and remote in his dark suit and white shirt. Although he was leanly built there was an unmistakable strength about the wide shoulders and broad, flatly muscled chest which tapered to narrow hips and long powerful legs, and Beth felt an unexpected quiver of awareness at his maleness which she ruthlessly suppressed.

'I do. You seem to be in a real predicament. Have you made any plans at all?'

'I wish I could, but it all seems such a muddle. That's why I came, to talk things through and hope that a solution would magically present itself, but that doesn't seem about to happen.' She smiled tightly, her eyes over-bright. 'It's going to take more than a chat to sort this out.'

'Perhaps.' He paused and she had the feeling that he was weighing up his words before he continued quietly, 'I think I may have a solution if you'd care to hear it.'

'You have?'

'Yes, although I don't know how you will feel about it.' He stared calmly at her and Beth felt a shiver of anticipation run along her veins.

'Then perhaps you'd better tell me what it is.'

'I do a great deal of my work here at the flat and for some time now I've been toying with the idea of employing a secretary part-time to help me out. It seems to me that you would fit the bill perfectly, Beth.'

'Me? But...' She stopped abruptly, the words drying up under the heat from the sudden surge of hope, and he continued smoothly as though she'd never spoken.

'Obviously your qualifications are just what I require, so my suggestion is that you take the job and, in view of your housing difficulties, that you come and live here. I would pay you a modest salary plus your board and lodgings. Once you're back on your feet and find somewhere else then we can review the situation, but it seems the ideal solution all around from where I'm standing. A sensible one, in fact.'

Sensible? No, it was crazy, totally and utterly crazy, and she should have rejected the idea at once. So why did she find herself hesitating? Why did she find herself staring into those cool grey eyes and searching for any reason under the sun why she should accept it? It didn't make any sense at all.

He interpreted her continued silence in a way she had never intended, smiling thinly as he walked to the desk and picked up a pen and started writing. 'I can understand your reluctance, Beth. Obviously you must be wary about coming here to live in my flat when you know nothing at all about me apart from my name and the fact that I like opera.' He held the paper out to her, his face impassive as he studied her. 'Here is a list of people for you to contact who will supply references about me. Please feel free to check them out. No sensible woman would commit herself to such a decision without ensuring she wasn't making a huge mistake. I'm no wild axe murderer, Beth, nor a white slave trafficker, and these highly respectable people will attest to that!'

She took the paper from him, barely glancing at the short list of names and addresses before she looked back at David with puzzlement in her eyes. 'But why, David? Why should you want to do so much for me? Oh, I know you say that you need help, but to offer me somewhere to live...' She shook her head. 'That can't be the only reason, needing help. You could chose anyone for that position, women who wouldn't impose on you by having to live in your home. Why are you doing this for me, David?'

'I've told you why, Beth. There are no strings attached. It's a genuine offer which would solve both our problems.' He set the pen back down, but not before she'd seen a flicker cross his face, a fleeting echo of old pain. She wished she had the courage to ask what had caused it, but events had taken their toll.

'I don't know what to say. I never expected...' She tailed off and took a shuddery little breath. 'Whatever I decide to do, I want you to know how grateful I am for the offer. You've been more than kind.'

'Kindness has nothing to do with it. I need help here, Beth, and you would fit the bill perfectly without my having to go through all the hassle of advertising the post and then interviewing the applicants.'

'You don't even know if I can type properly!' She gave a faint little smile, feeling warmed when he smiled slowly back at her.

'Can you?'

'Yes. Top speeds in college.'

'Well, then, there's no problem. Look, Beth, this offer is open to you for as long as you want it to be, even after you have the baby. There's room enough in the flat for both of you, but if you just want to take it for a few months to tide you over then that's fine with me. Just think about it...promise?'

She smiled at that, her face lighting up. 'You said that last time we met, made me promise to come to you if I needed help, and look where that's got you now!'

He laughed, taking her hand, his fingers hard and cool against her skin. 'I remember. I don't say things I don't mean. This plan would solve all your immediate problems and give you breathing space plus help me out.'

'It will probably give *you* problems you never even thought about!' She reached up to kiss him quickly on the cheek, her lips barely brushing his skin before she drew back. 'I shall think about it, David, long and hard, but only if you promise to do the same, and if you change your mind then I shall understand.'

'That won't happen. You can be assured of that.'

There was such steely certainty in his tone that for the first time in days Beth felt some of the gloom lift. The temptation to say yes there and then was great, but she stopped herself. It wouldn't be fair to accept then have him suddenly regret his offer after he'd had time to think it through.

'I'm tempted, David...very tempted, but...' She broke off, suddenly overwhelmed by his kindness. 'I shall be in touch and let you know what I decide.' She turned to hurry from the room, pausing in the doorway, the words of thanks dying on her lips as she saw him standing by the desk holding a framed photograph in his hands, his face set into rigid lines.

Beth crept from the room, trying to reconcile that grim-faced stranger with the man who had just offered her a job and a home. Which one was the real David Kane? She wished she knew. She glanced down at the sheet of paper he'd given her, skimming over the list of names and addresses of people who would testify as to his suitability as her employer and benefactor. Would any of them be able to tell her who exactly the real David Kane was? Somehow she doubted it. It was going to be something she would have to find out herself and suddenly, surprisingly, the idea of discovering the true nature of the man was intriguing.

CHAPTER THREE

'No, THIS is the right number. David is in the shower at present. Can I take a message or ask him to call you back when——?' Beth winced as the phone was slammed down, and set the receiver back with a wry grimace. She'd been at the flat just a couple of weeks and, although things were working remarkably well between her and David, she did seem to be having a disastrous effect on his social life. He was going to have some explaining to do from the sound of it . . . yet again!

'That for me?' He came down the hall, his blond hair still wet from the shower, his shirt hanging open over a pair of dark grey trousers, and Beth felt the little shiver of awareness she always felt when she saw him. He was so blatantly male that a woman would have to be blind not to appreciate his appeal.

'It was indeed. One very irate lady who was none too pleased to hear me answering the phone at this time of the morning.' She steeled herself, knowing what had to be said, yet dreading it. 'Look, David, I know my being here is making life difficult for you, so if you want me to find somewhere else then just say the word.'

He tossed the wet towel aside and came towards her, his face impassive as he watched her. 'Do you want to leave, Beth?'

'No! But neither do I want to cause you any upset. Your . . . your friends seem to have entirely the wrong idea why I'm here and it must be making life awkward for you.' Her face was flushed when she'd finished, but he seemed remarkably unperturbed by the idea.

'It's their problem what they think. I'm a free agent, Beth. I'm not accountable to anyone for my actions. Forget about it. Now is that coffee I can smell?'

Beth sighed, realising it was pointless to argue. One thing she had learned these past weeks was David's determination to have things his own way. Both in his business and private life he was cool and decisive, rarely displaying any emotion as he dealt with problems. She had come to admire the firm way he took control, the razor-sharp intelligence he displayed which cut through to the heart of a problem, even while she silently warned herself not to start relying on him too much to solve her problems. David wouldn't always be around to help her.

'I've just made a fresh pot. Would you like some toast to go with it?'

'You don't have to act as unpaid housekeeper as well, Beth. That wasn't why I asked you to stay here.'

There was an edge to his deep voice which irritated her. 'I know that! But making a slice or two of toast is hardly a union issue. I want to do my share around the flat, David.'

'Fair enough, but understand that it's your choice. I don't expect anything more from you than you are already doing. Frankly, your work has been of such a high standard that I feel I'm taking advantage of you by paying you so small a salary.'

'You've given me more than enough . . . a home and a job. Not many people would have done what you have.' She led the way along the hall into the kitchen and picked up the pot to pour the coffee then set it down again with a clatter. 'If anyone is being taken advantage of it's you! And why? Because I was too stupid to read the signs!' She slammed her hand down on the counter, fury shining in her eyes. Her emotions had run the gamut, moving from shock, despair and sorrow to this red-hot anger at what Andrew had done to her. 'I can't believe that I was stupid enough to be taken in like that! I should have realised there was something fishy about the way he acted, but I swallowed everything he told me, all that rot about how he couldn't see me of a weekend because his parents were elderly and they expected him to visit them, how he couldn't invite me back to where he lived because the chap he shared with left it looking like a pigsty! Do you realise that I actually admired him for it?' She spun round, glaring at David across the room, yet unaware that she was doing so because her thoughts were all turned inwards, plagued by the memories of how she'd been duped. 'I actually admired his devotion to his parents, his consideration of my feelings! I even admired him for the fact that he limited the number of nights we met so that he could work late at the office in the hope of getting promotion. How could any woman fall for that, the oldest story in the book, and not suspect a thing?'

Her face was flushed with temper, but he just watched her calmly. 'It's easy to be wise after the event. Now you can add it all up and see the pattern of his deceit, but then…' He shrugged. 'What does amaze me is your determination not to ask him for help. Why shouldn't he pay for what he's done, Beth?'

'You know why! I've explained it before. Why keep on asking the same question!'

'Because hopefully it will jolt you into seeing sense!' He started to button his shirt and tuck it into his trousers, his face set with a cold cynicism. 'You may rant and rail against what Andrew did, but how do you really feel about him? I think you are still in love with him and that's why you won't do anything that might harm him.'

'No! You're wrong. I hate him for what he has done. Do you hear me—hate him!' She rounded on him in fury, but he met her angry gaze levelly.

'I doubt that, otherwise you'd see the sense of what I'm trying to tell you. Why is it, Beth, that women are so blinded by their love that they can't see what fools they're being?'

'And why is it that men see love as a means to an end?' Her voice filled with bitterness. 'You try answering me that, David Kane, then I'll try answering your question!'

'You're not talking about love, though, Beth. You're talking about sexual desire, a powerful weapon in the wrong hands.' He sipped the coffee, his eyes like steel. 'Don't ever confuse the two. Men can be just as foolish under the influence of love, believe me.'

'That sounds like experience talking.' Beth picked up her own cup, chilled by the starkness on his face.

'It would be unlikely that I could reach the age of thirty without being stung by Cupid's arrow at some time.' He drank his coffee, faint amusement on his face, but Beth wasn't fooled. It would be easy to typecast David as the typical bachelor with a string of eager willing women at his disposal. Heaven knew she'd taken enough phone calls these past weeks to back that theory to the hilt. But every so often she would catch a glimpse of something in his face and realise that wasn't the case at all. What had happened in David's past? She wished she knew and yet, contrarily, hoped that she would never find out. She couldn't afford to get involved in his affairs when she had so many problems of her own.

She got up, suddenly anxious to change the subject. 'I imagine you're right. It would be strange. I'll make that toast now so how many slices do you want?'

'Just one, if you're sure you don't mind. I don't want to get too used to having you waiting on me, otherwise it will come as a nasty shock when you leave.'

Was that a subtle hint despite what he'd said? Her hands trembled as she cut slices off the loaf, but she tried her hardest to keep the fear from her voice. 'I have been looking for somewhere else to live, David, but so far I've not found anywhere suitable. Either they're too expensive or too run-down, but I am really trying, I assure you.'

'I didn't mean that! Dammit, Beth, have I asked you to find somewhere else? Well, have I? You know very well that I told you that you could stay here as long as you wanted to.'

He sounded so angry that her voice wavered. 'I . . . I know that but I thought maybe . . . well, that maybe you had decided it wasn't working out.'

'It's working just fine. Better than I could have anticipated. And the last thing I expect is that you should go traipsing the streets in your condition.' His eyes dropped to the faint swell of her stomach and Beth felt heat warm her cheeks as she became immediately conscious of the button at the top of her trousers which she'd had to leave unfastened to accommodate her increasing waistline.

She turned away, busying herself with putting the bread into the toaster. She still hadn't come to terms completely with her pregnancy, still hadn't fully accepted that she was carrying a child. She could see the gradual changes in her body—the thickening of her waistline, the increased fullness of her breasts—and they embarrassed her. Maybe it would have been different if Andrew had been free to marry her. Then she would have felt proud that their love had created this child, but all she could feel as yet was a sense of guilt.

'Let's have no more talk about you looking for a flat, eh? You are welcome here for as long as you choose to stay. Understand?'

She nodded, keeping her face averted. 'Yes. Thank you, but it still doesn't seem fair that you should be inconvenienced because of my stupid mistake.'

'Leave me to worry about being inconvenienced or not. And as for it being your mistake . . .' He broke off, obviously trying to curb an uncharacteristic flash of anger. 'From where I'm standing it seems that Andrew is the one who made the biggest mistake by lying to you, and I'm damned sure he hasn't lost a night's sleep over it all!'

Minutes before she had been the one berating Andrew, yet now it stung to hear David say such things. 'How do you know? You're passing judgement when you have no idea how he feels! Maybe he wanted to contact me, but felt that it would be kinder to leave well alone.'

'Kinder? He lied to you, used you, and then abandoned you, and you think he's been kind? Didn't I say that love makes a woman blind?' He picked up the cup and drained the coffee from it, then looked back at her with contempt. 'You need to sort out exactly what you feel for Andrew, and to do that you have to stop fooling yourself into thinking that he cares a jot about you because frankly, Beth, from where I'm standing there's little evidence of it!'

He left without another word and Beth turned back to the toast, knowing in her heart that he was right. Her emotions had been in such a muddle these past weeks, but somehow she had to decide once and for all what she really felt. She had loved Andrew so much that it seemed impossible that love could change so soon and yet . . .

She closed her eyes, trying to summon up a mental image of Andrew and recall the way he had made her feel when they were together, but for some reason his image wouldn't take shape. When she closed her eyes all she could see was the face of a man with blond hair and eyes like steel . . .

She was tired. Spurred on by the strangely unsettling experience, Beth had finished her work then set about checking all the agencies she could find in the hope of finding somewhere to stay, but to no avail. The only room available in her price range had been on the sixth floor of a run-down building and common sense told her that she would never manage the steep flights of stairs in a few months' time.

With a weary sigh she let herself into the flat and closed the door, wondering warily if David was home yet. She felt too tired to cope with another confrontation yet neither did she feel like smoothing things over with an apology. In her opinion he was as much to blame for their disagreement as she was!

The sudden sharp ring of the bell startled her and she spun round, feeling her head swirl with dizziness at the unguarded movement. Fighting against it, she opened the door then had to cling tightly to the frame for support as the room gave another alarming tilt.

'Surprise, David! Ohhh!'

The woman was beautiful; Beth just had time to notice that one fact before concern crossed the woman's face as she noticed the waxen pallor of Beth's skin and the way she was clinging grimly to the woodwork.

'Are you all right? You look dreadful. Let me help you.' She slipped an arm round Beth's waist as she stepped inside and helped her back to the sitting-room to settle her in a chair. 'Stay right there. I'll get you a glass of water.'

She hurried from the room, leaving a tantalising drift of some exotic perfume lingering in the air. Who was she? She obviously knew David and just as obviously knew her way round the flat, yet there had been surprise rather than animosity on her face when she'd seen Beth at the door.

'Here you are. Can you manage to sit up? Better let me help you.' The woman hurried back into the room and helped Beth up against the cushions before handing her the glass. Beth took a sip of the water, feeling the faintness receding. She set the glass down then ran a hand over her hair to smooth the wispy curls into place.

'Feeling better? It's rotten when you go dizzy like that. Has it happened to you before?'

Beth nodded, glancing unthinkingly down at the slight swell of her stomach where her waistband was unbuttoned, and heard the stranger gasp. Curious as to the reason for it, she looked at her in time to surprise an expression of shock on her face before she managed to collect herself and smile apologetically at Beth.

'I'm sorry. You must think me terribly rude. It was just a surprise. I had no idea, you see.'

'No idea about what?' Beth tried to follow the strange shift in the conversation, but it was difficult when she was working at such a disadvantage.

'About the baby, of course. When is it due? It must be a while yet.' The woman sat down and crossed long, slender legs, smiling warmly at Beth. She really was exceptionally beautiful with her porcelain-fine skin, deep green eyes and thick, rich red hair which fell in glossy waves to her shoulders.

Beth studied her for a long moment, wondering if there wasn't something familiar about her face, before forcing her attention back to the question that had been asked. 'Some time in early April.'

'You must be so excited.' The woman laughed, her face lighting up. 'I've not long ago had my second child, another girl, in fact. She'll be four months old soon and I feel so lucky to have her. What are you hoping for, a boy or a girl?'

'I... I haven't really thought about it.' Beth took a deep breath, realising that she had to say something before the situation became even more awkward. 'Look, I'm very sorry, but I'm rather in the dark. Who are you?'

Something flashed in the woman's eyes, a mixture of pain and regret, then abruptly she stood up and walked to the window to stare out over the trees just as Beth had done that time when David had offered her the job and a place to live. The comparison between her and the other woman was so stark that Beth felt a sharp little tug of pain. Set alongside her, she would pale into insignificance, and she was woman enough to dislike the idea.

'It's I who should apologise. I just assumed that you would know who I am, but why should you?' She turned, a brilliant yet artificial smile on her lips. 'I'm Maggie Kane.'

'Maggie Kane... then you must be David's...' Beth couldn't seem to get the words out as shock enveloped her.

'That's right: David's sister-in-law. I'm married to his brother, Matthew, although I wouldn't be at all surprised if he hasn't said much about either of us.'

Beth swallowed hard, unwilling to admit that she'd been terrified of what Maggie had been about to say. For a moment there she'd imagined that she was going to claim to be David's wife, and she couldn't have borne the shock of that, of having history repeat itself. 'I'm afraid David hasn't mentioned you to me.' She stood up, feeling clumsy and ill at ease. 'I'm Beth Thomas.'

'Thomas? Then you and David aren't...?' Maggie stopped, glancing pointedly at Beth's stomach, and Beth felt colour flare in her face.

'No! Look, I think it's time that I did some explaining now. David and I aren't——'

'Married. And Beth feels very self-conscious about her present state. We shall have to do something about it, I think.'

Beth hadn't heard the door opening and she jumped nervously as David suddenly appeared. He came over to where she was standing and slid an arm around her shoulders. Beth flinched and started to move away, then stopped when his hand fastened on her shoulder to hold her by his side. What was going on here? He had never really touched her before, yet now the way his arm was resting around her shoulders implied a degree of intimacy which made her uneasy.

'How have you been, Maggie?' His voice was cool, so cool that Beth forgot her unease in sheer surprise. This was his brother's wife so surely she should warrant a touch more warmth than that coldly polite enquiry?

'Fine. And how about you, David? I hear that the business is doing very well. You must be pleased.'

'Naturally. It makes all the hard work worth while.' His fingers tightened on Beth's shoulder for a moment before he moved away to pour himself a large glass of whisky. Beth's eyes widened; David never drank this early in the day and definitely never filled a glass that full. What was wrong with him?

'Would you like a drink, Maggie?' he offered politely.

Maggie shook her head. 'I'd better not. The baby wouldn't appreciate it. I'm still nursing her.'

David's face tightened, then he looked away as he busied himself adding ice to his glass. 'I heard you'd had another child. Congratulations.'

'Thank you. Another girl. Janey was thrilled to have a little sister. We called her Elizabeth.' She turned to Beth with something like relief, as though she was glad to shift the conversation round to her. 'Is that your real name too?'

Beth shook her head, glancing quickly from Maggie's strained face to David's equally set one. She felt like an onlooker standing in the wings watching a play unfold step by slow, painful step. What had happened in this family to make the meeting between Maggie and David so tense? 'No. I was actually christened Beth. It's not a diminutive. But I must say that I like the name Elizabeth. It has a lovely sound to it.'

She was talking to cover the silence and Maggie shot her a grateful look. 'That's what Matthew and I thought, too. We spent ages trying to find a name we could both agree on then finally arrived at that. That's part of the fun of having a baby, as you must well know yourselves . . . choosing the name.'

It was obvious what she thought and Beth tried again to set the record straight. 'Oh, but this baby isn't——'

'Isn't going to have a name from the way things are going. It is surprisingly difficult to agree on one, isn't it, Beth?'

Beth gaped at him in surprise. They had never discussed baby's names, had never discussed anything apart from the practicalities involved in her sharing the flat.

'Then you and Matthew must be more alike than I thought! He was worse than me, rejecting one name after another.'

There was warmth in Maggie's voice, but it wasn't echoed in David's. 'I doubt my dear brother would appreciate you making the comparison between us, Maggie.'

'He's changed, David. Really he has. I . . . I wish you two would meet and try to patch things up.' Maggie glanced at Beth, a faint hope showing on her face. 'And this could be the ideal opportunity.'

David followed the look, frowning as he too stared at Beth. 'There would never be an ideal opportunity and you know it, Maggie. There's too much water under the bridge for Matthew and me ever to get together again.'

'I wish you wouldn't say that! It's wrong for two brothers to be at odds like this.'

'It's life, Maggie, and you can't change it.' He lifted the glass and took a long swallow of the whisky. Beth caught her breath at the expression which showed so fleetingly on his face. Was this what had caused him so much pain, this disagreement with his brother?

'I won't argue with you.' Maggie's voice was soft, her eyes almost pleading. 'I didn't come here for that. I came to tell you that we're moving back to

London. There have been some problems with the practice and Matthew feels that it's time he was back here in control once more. You've probably heard rumours about it.'

He shook his head, light bouncing off the smooth golden hair which lay close to his well-shaped head. He looked relaxed as he stood there holding the glass, but Beth could sense the tension in him. Instinctively she edged closer to him, not really understanding why she felt he needed her support at that moment. He shot her a quick glance then slowly held out his hand. Beth took the last couple of steps and slid her hand into his, feeling the way his fingers tightened around hers.

'I don't have time to listen to rumours, Maggie, especially not those about things which no longer concern me. That part of my life is past and I don't miss it.'

Maggie glanced at them, her eyes dropping to where Beth's hand lay in his, and Beth had the strangest feeling that she saw relief on the other woman's face.

'I'm sure you don't. Not now that you have so many other things to think about. I'm so pleased for you both. Congratulations.'

Was it honesty that prompted her to speak? Beth had no idea, but suddenly she couldn't stand this a moment longer. 'Look, Maggie, I don't know what you think is——'

She got no further, the words stopped on her lips as David pulled her round and kissed her hard on the mouth. Beth shuddered, feeling the touch of his lips like a brand. When he let her go she stared at him, shock flaring in the depths of her eyes.

'Stop it, Beth. Maggie isn't going to sit in judgement on you. You're far too sensitive.'

'Of course I'm not!' Maggie smiled, smoothing the skirt of her suit. 'Anyway, I have to go. I just wanted to let you know that we're back so it wouldn't come as a shock if you ran across Matthew.' She held her hand out to Beth, her green eyes filled with a very genuine warmth. 'It has been lovely meeting you, Beth. I hope we shall get the chance to get to know one another better.'

Beth took her hand, murmuring some pleasantry she was scarcely aware of. All she could think of, feel, taste was the touch of David's mouth on hers for those brief seconds. She closed her eyes, using the few minutes it took for him to see Maggie to the door to try to get herself back under control again, but when he came back into the room she couldn't stop the shiver which ran hotly along her veins.

'David, I . . .' It was difficult to speak around the knot of tension, but she had to try. 'What was going on just now? Why did you allow Maggie to think the . . . the baby is yours?' Her face flamed at the very idea and he studied her for a moment before calmly picking up the glass again.

'It seemed easier than to start explaining the truth.'

'"Easier"? You allowed her to think that you are the father of this child and you call that "easier"?' She clenched her fists until her knuckles gleamed white. 'Who gave you the right to do that? What sort of game are you playing?'

'Why should I be playing at anything? Maggie made a natural assumption and it didn't seem worth the effort to explain the true facts to her.'

'Not worth the effort?' Fury rose in a flash, consuming her, filling her with fire. 'You can't go around lying to people about something like this!'

'Why not? It's obvious that you are embarrassed about being pregnant so what was I supposed to do? Start going into all the unsavoury details with a stranger?'

'But she isn't a stranger to you! Dammit, David, she's your brother's wife. She deserves to be told the truth!'

'Does she?' For a moment there was naked fury on his face and Beth took an unconscious step backwards. Then, just as swiftly, the mask slid back into place and he was once more David, smooth, urbane, master of his emotions.

'I told Maggie exactly what she wanted to hear, Beth. Perhaps I told her something which would be the solution to all our problems.'

'What? I don't understand.'

He laughed shortly and set the glass down before moving closer to look directly into her eyes. 'Think about it, then. Wouldn't it solve your problems if you were married and had someone to lean on in the coming months? So why not marry me, Beth? We've already proved that we can live together in some degree of harmony and that's more than I could say for most women.'

'Marry you? I . . . but . . . No!' She backed away, anger glittering in her eyes. 'If this is some kind of a joke, David Kane, then it's in very poor taste!'

'It's not a joke.' He came after her. 'You need someone to support you and the child, and, if you are honest, you need the security that marriage can give you. I can offer you both.'

'But why? What do you stand to gain from this?' She laughed shrilly. 'No one is that much of a Good Samaritan!'

'Of course not. I have my reasons, Beth.' He turned away to drop down into one of the chairs, his face composed.

'And have you any intention of explaining what they are?' She drew in a shuddery little breath, striving for calm, for understanding, for any single thing that would help her make sense of the offer, and slowly it came to her. 'Are you doing this because it will help heal the rift between you and your brother somehow?'

His face closed and he stared down at the floor for a moment before lifting his eyes back to hers. 'Partly. Maggie was right: it is time this feud was ended, especially in view of the fact that they're back in London. Our paths are bound to cross from time to time.'

What was he holding back? Beth knew there was something, but she couldn't discern much from his expression. 'I may be obtuse, but how will marrying me help end this feud? I shouldn't have imagined it would make one iota of difference to you or your brother or the quarrel you've had in the past!'

'I'm afraid I'm not prepared to go into details at present. What happened between Matthew and me is our business, no one else's.'

'Not even mine? Not even when you're proposing marriage to me to help clear it all up? Come on, David, don't you think I have a right to know all the facts?' Anger and a strange hurt rippled through her at his refusal to tell her the truth.

'I've told you all I intend to tell you, Beth. Just take my word for it that marriage between us would be the ideal solution to all our problems. I can't make a fairer offer than that.'

His arrogance almost took her breath away. 'Then I'm afraid that I shall have to turn your offer down! I've already made one huge error in my life and I'll be damned if I'll leap blindly into making another!' She turned to hurry from the room, feeling her heart beating painfully. Marry David Kane? Marry a man who refused to tell her the real truth about why he should wish such a thing? The idea should have shocked her; the fact that it didn't shocked her even more. Just for a moment there before she'd come to her senses she'd been almost tempted to accept!

'Promise me that you will at least think about what I've said, Beth?' His voice was deep and compelling, drawing her to a halt when all she wanted was to run before common sense fled in the face of temptation. Had he known exactly what to say to make her pause, used the very words—the only ones—that would stop her from dismissing his offer right away once she'd calmed down? Probably. Yet even admitting it couldn't prevent her from turning back.

'Promise me, Beth?' He held her gaze across the room, his eyes deep and shadowed, and Beth knew then that she was lost. Shc closed her eyes, desperately trying to think of all the sane and sensible reasons why she should tell him to go to hell, but all that came into her mind was how he looked sitting in that chair, watching her and waiting.

'Yes. I promise.' It was little more than a whisper, yet the words echoed in the silence and lingered long after she'd fled from the room.

CHAPTER FOUR

HUNGER drove Beth from her room in the early hours of the morning. She'd spent the time since she'd left David trying to think what to do, but there was no easy answer. Now the hollow feeling in her stomach had her creeping along the hall and into the kitchen.

She made herself a sandwich then sat down at the table to eat it, but after only a few bites found that her appetite had disappeared. Setting the bread back on to the plate, she sat staring into space, going back over everything that had been said as she'd done a hundred times already. There was no way she could accept such an offer as David had made, yet in her heart she knew that she was tempted to and that scared her. She didn't want to let herself become too fond of David. That was a route to even more heartache.

'Are you all right?' His voice was soft, but Beth still jumped when he spoke. She swung round, feeling the colour flare in her face when she found him standing in the doorway watching her.

'I...I'm fine. I was hungry so I came to make something to eat.' She picked up the sandwich and took a bite, then had to force herself to chew it.

'No wonder. You should be more careful, Beth. You can't afford to skip meals at present.' He came further into the room and opened the fridge to pour himself a glass of milk, leaning a hip against the worktop as he drank it slowly, his grey eyes intent as he watched her over the rim of the glass.

Beth looked away, putting the sandwich down to tear at the crust with nervous fingers. If only she knew what he was really thinking then maybe she would know how to handle this situation, but it was impossible to read anything in the coolly level gaze.

'Have you thought about my offer, Beth?'

She nodded, her hair swirling against the navy silk of her housecoat, the red-gold curls glowing in the bright electric light. 'Yes. I've done little else but think about it.'

'And what have you decided?' There was no inflexion in his deep voice. To an outsider he might have been asking anything, not asking if she'd decided to marry him, and it stung.

'That it's totally ridiculous. Maybe if you told me the whole truth then I could find the idea more acceptable, but…' She straightened, her eyes overbright with a combination of annoyance and tiredness. 'How will marrying me solve your problems, David?'

'Just accept that it will, Beth. Is that too much to ask in the circumstances?'

'What circumstances?'

He set the glass down, hunching his shoulders as he slipped his hands into his pockets. He was still wearing his suit trousers although he had shed the jacket, and Beth could see the faint ripple of muscles under the fine fabric of his pale blue shirt. She looked away, strangely disturbed by the sight, feeling a tightness in her chest.

'In view of the fact that I offered you a job and somewhere to live quite unconditionally. I didn't go delving into your past, Beth. Is it too much to expect the same courtesy from you?'

Beth flushed, hating him for reminding her so pointedly of all she owed him. 'This is different!'

'In which way? It's just another solution to your problems and it will go a long way towards easing my life.'

He was inching her back into a corner, using that cool, clear logic to confuse the real issue at stake, playing on the fact that she felt beholden to him for all he'd done. 'But this isn't just a business proposition! You're talking about marriage and all that implies! Maybe this isn't to be a normal arrangement . . .' She broke off, her face going pale. 'I take it that you don't intend this marriage to be a normal one? I . . . I may have misunderstood before.'

He came over to the table and pulled out a chair. 'It can be whatever you want it to be, Beth.'

'And what's that supposed to mean?' She laughed bitterly. 'Stop playing games, David. I'm far too tired to cope with that. Did you or did you not intend this marriage to be a real one?'

'If by that you are asking if I expect you to sleep with me, then no. That wasn't what I intended.' He caught her eyes, the lean planes of his face seemingly carved from stone. 'I never intended that you should jump into bed with me as some sort of a payment, Beth. I'm well aware of how you feel about Andrew.'

'Payment? Fine payment it would be in my present state!' She glanced down at her thickening waistline, her eyes sparkling with unshed tears. 'I'm hardly the catch of the year, am I?'

'Stop that!' He caught her chin to lift her head so that he could look deep into her eyes, and Beth was shocked to see anger burning in his. 'You are a beautiful woman, Beth. Being pregnant doesn't change that fact.'

She smiled shakily, more disturbed by the look and the touch of his fingers then she cared to admit. 'You're just saying that. I'm not beautiful. Maggie is beautiful, so you should be able to see the difference by comparing us.'

His fingers contracted, making her wince as they bruised her flesh before he let her go. 'Let's leave Maggie out of this. She doesn't concern either of us right now.' He looked past her and Beth had the sudden, strangest feeling that he was lost in thought and bitter thought at that. He seemed to collect himself all at once, his face smoothing out. 'I want you to marry me, Beth, because it would be the perfect solution all round. There is nothing sinister about my reasons for suggesting it, just a long-overdue desire to clear the air once and for all, to end an old grievance before anyone else gets hurt. I don't want to pressurise you, but you should look at this from a rational viewpoint. If Andrew had been free then none of this would be happening. But he is married, and presumably, from what happened that first time we met, fully intending to stay that way. I will provide for you and the child for however long you need. It's as simple as that.'

'"Simple"? It isn't "simple"! The whole idea is full of pitfalls!' She glared back at him, but he seemed unmoved and she hurried on, desperate to make him understand, desperate to make it clear inside her own head why she couldn't accept. 'We hardly know one another. Who's to say if we can live together in any degree of harmony? A couple of weeks here in the flat is hardly any guarantee!'

'No? From where I'm standing it seems a reasonable bet. You aren't a difficult person to have around, Beth.'

She ignored the deliberate compliment, racking her brain for more reasons, good ones this time. 'But what happens if circumstances change and you meet someone you *really* want to marry? There will be all the delay of obtaining a divorce.'

'That won't happen.' He stood up to walk over to the sink to wash the milky glass, a stiffness to his actions as he swirled water round and round the bowl.

'How can you be sure? Life doesn't always follow the route we plan. I know that.'

He turned round, drying his hands on a towel. 'Maybe not, but I can state quite categorically that love is the last thing I'm looking for from life.'

Beth shivered, chilled to the bone by the coldness of the response. 'I guess I can second that. Love isn't something I'm looking for after what's happened.'

'Then doesn't it make even more sense that you should agree? Look, Beth, you know you're embarrassed by your present state. I might not be the child's father, but marrying me will help you cope more easily with the coming months, plus it will make my life far simpler.'

'Will it?'

'Yes. Come on, Beth. What have you got to lose?'

She smiled shakily, wishing he weren't so persuasive. He knew exactly how to cut right through all her objections. 'On the surface I haven't anything to lose, but I'm not so sure about you.'

'Leave me to worry about that. So... what do you say? Yes or no?'

'I...' She swallowed hard, her heart pounding so fast that she felt it would explode. What should she say? 'Yes' seemed like every sort of madness, yet...

She closed her eyes, trying desperately to think what to do. If circumstances had been different then this would never have been necessary, but Andrew was part of her past and now there was only David who seemed to care what became of her. How could she refuse his offer and yet continue living in the flat and working for him? She would have to leave and suddenly the thought of never seeing him again made it all crystal-clear.

'Yes.' It came out as a whisper and she repeated it, afraid that he might not have heard. 'Yes!'

'Good.' He came and took her hands to draw her to her feet. 'You won't regret it, Beth.'

She tried to smile, but her mouth felt stiff as the shock of what she'd done hit her. 'I hope not. But you must promise me one thing, David. That if you meet someone else you will tell me. I don't ever want to ruin your happiness and have you regret what you've done.'

'That won't happen, but, if it will set your mind at rest, then yes.' He kissed her gently on the cheek, his touch almost impersonal.

Beth closed her eyes, letting herself lean against him for a moment as she drew on his strength before she moved away. She hurried from the room, her eyes shadowed with doubts despite her acceptance. David had said that it would be up to her which direction the marriage took, but she must never lose sight of the reasons why he had asked her to marry him in the first place. If she hadn't been alone and pregnant and he hadn't seen it as a way to end the quarrel with his brother then it would never have taken place. She must never let herself start imagining that he had asked her because he *cared*.

The dress was exquisite. Pale creamy silk, it fell in soft folds to skim the fullness of her breasts and drape softly over the slight swell of her stomach.

Beth stared at herself in the long mirror, touching a hand to the silky strands of her hair which floated around her shoulders. David had asked her to wear her hair down and she had readily agreed, but now she wondered if it had been a mistake. She looked young and strangely innocent in this dress with her soft curls drifting around her face, but she knew she wasn't that. She had lost her innocence and the child she was carrying was testimony to that. Her whole appearance was a sham just as this wedding was a sham. She must have been mad to agree to go through with it!

Panic rose inside her, hot and fierce, and she spun away from the mirror. She had to stop this now, had to find David and tell him that she couldn't go through with the wedding before it was too late.

She half ran from the room, stumbling as the heel of one cream leather shoc caught on the hall rug. She slowed, listening to the silence as she wondered where David was, then saw him as she came level with the sitting-room door.

He was standing staring into the empty fire-grate with an expression on his face which made the words die on her lips. What was he thinking about? Beth had no idea yet she experienced a deep reluctance to intrude on his privacy.

He must have sensed her presence in the doorway because he turned suddenly, his gaze skimming her in one long, assessing look which made a *frisson* run down her spine.

'You look lovely, Beth.' There was no mistaking the genuine appreciation in his tone and she was woman enough to feel a rush of pleasure at the compliment although she wouldn't let it deter her from what she had to say.

'Thank you.' She moved further into the room, glancing nervously around, wondering where to start, but he took the initiative from her.

'Cold feet, Beth?'

There was cool amusement in his voice and she stiffened. 'Yes, if you want the truth! Look, David, I know we've been through all this before, but I'm still not sure we are doing the right thing.'

'It's just bridal nerves, Beth. I imagine most women feel like that on their wedding day. It's quite normal.'

'But this isn't a normal wedding!' His attitude annoyed her intensely. 'Stop trying to make this out to be something it isn't, David!'

'This is our wedding day. That's a fact just as it's a fact that you are experiencing last-minute doubts the same as dozens of other women before you. What's so strange about that?'

'Nothing. But this marriage is hardly the norm, is it?' She glared at him, close to tears at his deliberate refusal to understand what she meant.

'Perhaps not, but that doesn't make it wrong. What is really troubling you, Beth? The fact that we aren't in love? I'd say that was a plus factor. Love doesn't guarantee happiness as you very well know.'

He was never cruel and that he should be so now devastated her. Tears shone like diamonds on her lashes as she faced him across the room. 'That was a horrible thing to say. How could you, David? Do you imagine this is easy? I loved Andrew and the fact that it didn't work out for us was just a tragic mistake.'

'A mistake?' He smiled harshly as he came towards her. 'It might have been a mistake on your behalf, Beth, but it was hardly a mistake on his! He knew exactly what he was doing and the risks he was taking right from the start. The trouble is that he wasn't the one to get hurt. Andrew used you all along the line and don't ever forget it!'

'No!' She backed away from him, her face going pale. 'He couldn't have foreseen that I would get pregnant. Andrew loved me... he did!'

'So he loved you, did he? Loved you so much that he was willing to risk your unhappiness by asking you out when he knew he was married? Loved you so much that he took no precautions to ensure you didn't get pregnant? It doesn't sound like love to me. It sounds like lust. Don't confuse the two.'

'How can you say that? You know nothing about our relationship. It wasn't lust! He... oh!' She stopped abruptly, her breath catching as he caught her to him and held her tightly, his hand splayed across the hollow of her back so that she was brought into abrupt contact with his muscled body. Just for a second shock kept her immobile, then she began to struggle, pushing wildly at the steely strength of his arms.

'Let me go! What do you think you're doing?'

'Attempting to show you the difference between those two emotions.' He slid a hand behind her head, tugging gently but insistently at her hair so that she was forced to tilt her head back. 'You're old enough to realise that there is a difference, Beth.'

His mouth came down as he took her lips in a kiss which sent a shiver of pure hot fire sliding along her veins. Beth stilled at once, her whole body going rigid with shock. Nothing had prepared her for this, forewarned her that just the touch of David's mouth on hers could make her burn with a heat she'd never felt before. When his hand slid up to tilt her face so that he could deepen the kiss, Beth made no move to break away. She felt boneless, melting under the warmth of his mouth and the strange curling sensations rippling hotly along her veins.

When his mouth slid away from hers, she moaned softly, turning her head to recapture his lips then shuddering as he began to skim a shower of kisses along the curve of her jaw to the hollow of her neck. Slowly, gently, he traced the delicate hollow with his tongue before moving on to nibble at the lobe of her ear in a way which stole what little remaining strength she had from her so that she trembled against him. He caught her even closer, steadying her against his strength as he continued the assault on her senses by taking her mouth again in a long, drugging kiss, and everything ceased to exist apart from the feel of his mouth on hers and the hot, delicious magic they were creating together.

Slowly he drew back, holding her steady as he felt the shudders which racked her, his hand smoothing the silky disarray he'd made of her hair. 'Do you see now, Beth, how easily desire can spring up between a man and a woman, but it isn't love? The two don't always have to go together.'

Beth pulled away, her face pale as she turned her back on him so that he wouldn't see the shock in her eyes. She loved Andrew so how could she feel this way about another man? How could the touch of David's mouth on hers make her feel as though she'd never been kissed before.

'If we're going to get to the Register Office on time then we shall have to leave now. Are you ready?'

Was she? Was she ready to take a step which could turn out to be a huge mistake? But if she refused to go through with it then there would never be a second chance. David would never ask her again, she knew that, and the thought frightened her even more. She should have hated him for what he'd done in trying to teach her such a bitter lesson, should have loathed the fact that his kiss had wiped away the memory of Andrew's kisses, yet, as she turned to look at him standing quietly waiting for an answer, she knew that wasn't how she felt at all.

Right or wrong, she couldn't imagine life without David now.

'Yes.'

He smiled suddenly, the aloofness fading as he held out his hand to her. 'You won't regret it, Beth.'

She slid her hand into his, shivering despite the warmth of his fingers. Someone walking over her grave, or a premonition of things to come? She had no idea. All she could do now that she had given him her answer was pray that it would turn out right in the end. The last thing she wanted was to get hurt again, and something told her that David had far more power to hurt than he should.

CHAPTER FIVE

'THANK you, Mrs Kane. Here's your card and your receipt. Mrs Kane?'

Beth jumped, taking the cheque card from the assistant with a murmur of thanks. She picked up her parcel and made her way from the counter, wondering when she would ever get used to being called by that name. They had been married for almost a month now, but she didn't feel any different from how she'd felt before. David treated her with an unfailing courtesy, but that was it. They could be two polite strangers working together and sharing a flat, yet what more did she expect? She knew why he had asked her to marry him and should be glad that he was keeping to the guidelines. So why did she sometimes find herself watching him and wishing for something more?

'Beth! It is you, isn't it?'

She turned when she heard her name being called, smiling as she recognised the beautiful redhead hurrying towards her through the crowd. 'Hello, Maggie. How are you?'

'Fine. And how about you?' Maggie laughed, her green eyes sparkling with mischief as she glanced pointedly at Beth's stomach. 'Starting to bloom from the look of it.'

Beth returned the smile, unable to feel uncomfortable at Maggie's good-natured teasing. David had been right about it being easier for her now that she was married. She could accept her pregnancy so much better. Perhaps it was old-fashioned, but it had been the way she had been brought up and it was difficult to change such ingrained views.

'I feel fine, thank you. Well, maybe that's an exaggeration. Most days I feel fine until I look in the mirror and see what I'm starting to look like!'

Maggie laughed again, slipping a hand through Beth's arm to draw her away from the crowds milling between the racks of clothes. 'I know exactly what you mean. What are you now . . . four . . . four and a half months pregnant? This is the worst stage, believe me. You've reached the point when nothing fits yet you aren't yet big enough to fill out all those voluminous maternity dresses!'

'Precisely. Still, I suppose I can look at you and hope. You did say that you'd had a baby just a few months ago?'

'I did indeed, and you *will* get your figure back. Mind you, I've still got a few pounds to lose before I'm down to my usual weight. I shall have to try harder to cut out all those tempting little goodies, but not right now. Now I'm going to whisk you upstairs and buy you coffee and a slice of the most sinfully delicious fresh-cream gâteau you've ever tasted. And I won't take no for an answer!'

'Who's arguing? I'd just about finished here anyway.' Beth followed the other woman through the crowd to the lift, clutching the paper parcel in her hand.

'Finished? With only one parcel? Matthew would start worrying that I was ill if I went shopping and came home with that!' Maggie pressed the button to summon the lift, raising an amused brow as she studied the package.

'Oh, I didn't want to buy much. I can't afford…' Beth broke off, colouring as she realised how it must sound. Apart from the household budget she'd not touched a penny of David's money, not even the salary he continued to pay her for working as his secretary. She was saving all she could to buy things for the baby when it arrived. She couldn't expect David to pay for any of that, despite what he had said. This child was her responsibility, not his. It surprised her, suddenly, just how much that thought hurt. What would it have been like if she'd been having David's child, not Andrew's?

'David is a wealthy man, Beth. He is also one of the kindest, most generous people I've ever met. He would be horrified to think that you are skimping on things you need.'

Maggie's voice drew her back to the present and thankfully Beth pushed the unsettling thoughts to the very back of her mind. 'I know. But I want to maintain my independence for as long as I can.'

Maggie pressed the button for the third floor. 'I can understand that, but take it from one who knows and don't make the mistake of trying to be too independent. David needs to be involved with his child from the outset.'

There was a wealth of sadness in Maggie's voice, but Beth scarcely heard it, overcome by guilt. Obviously David had still told no one, not even his family, the truth about the baby, so what was she supposed to do? Go along with the lie or confess? He hadn't invited his brother or Maggie to the wedding. It had been a low-key affair with just a couple of David's friends to act as witnesses although Beth knew that he telephoned his mother to tell her. Now it put her in an intolerable situation. She could either tell Maggie the truth to ease her conscience, and risk David's anger, or continue with the deception.

'Shall we sit by the window? There's a good view across the roof-tops from there.' Maggie led the way to a free table and sat down, the smile fading as she studied Beth for a moment. 'Matthew's mother told us about the wedding, Beth. I was sorry that we couldn't be there, but you must know that I wish you both all the luck in the world.'

'Thank you. I . . . I'm sorry you couldn't be there too, Maggie, but . . .' She trailed off, wondering what to say to cover the awkward little moment, but Maggie seemed to understand.

'But things are still fraught between those two pig-headed men of ours. Oh, I understand how it is, Beth. Who better, in fact?' She reached in her bag for a tissue and blew her nose, a suspicious trace of brightness in her green eyes. 'One of these days I'm going to knock their silly heads together in the hope that it will knock some sense into them both!'

It sounded such an unlikely remedy that Beth laughed out loud. 'If your Matthew is anything like David then I doubt even that would achieve anything! Still, if it's any consolation David did say something about it being time to end this feud so maybe they will get around to it soon.'

'Did he indeed? Well, that is encouraging.'

'Yes. He seemed to think marrying me could help although I have no idea why.' Beth waited, holding her breath to hear what Maggie might say, but all she did was smile a trifle sadly.

'I think it will take more than that unfortunately. They need to talk to each other and finally straighten things out, but neither of them will take the first step. The old Kane stubbornness raising its ugly head as usual. They would hate me for saying it, but deep down they are so alike!'

'What does Matthew do? Is he in business too?'

'He's a barrister. He runs the family law firm.'

'Law? But David told me that he used to practise law. Did they work together?' There was open curiosity in Beth's voice at the unexpected revelation.

'They did. It was expected of them that they would follow in their father's footsteps, but David was never truly happy in that environment. When . . . when something happened that made it impossible for them to continue working together, he left and started his furniture-design business.'

'I see. And this thing that happened, is that what caused this rift between them?'

'Yes.' Maggie smiled with a touch of apology. 'Don't ask me about it, Beth. It's not something I can tell you about. You must ask David.'

She picked up the menu and reluctantly Beth let the subject drop, although it was impossible to dismiss it from her mind. It should have been enough that she had the security of a home and a job, a means of support for herself and the baby, but in her heart she knew it wasn't. She wanted to know how David's marrying her would ease a situation that had apparently existed for some time. Perhaps if she could understand that then she could start to share in his life more fully.

It was a tantalising thought, one that stayed with her while they drank their coffee and chatted. When they left the coffee bar they took the lift to the ground floor, stopping to one side of the revolving doors to say their goodbyes.

'Thanks for the coffee, Maggie. I enjoyed it and the chat.'

'So did I. We must do it again, in fact. Or, better still, make arrangements for you to come and meet my two horrors.'

'I'd love that, but...' She tailed off uncertainly. 'Would it be a good idea though? I mean, what would Matthew have to say about your inviting me round?'

'I have no idea, and frankly I don't care! It's time this was resolved once and for all. Look, Beth, I was planning on asking this anyway, but now seems like the perfect time. Elizabeth is being christened in a couple of weeks' time and I want you to stand as one of her godmothers.'

'Me? I don't know what to say.' Beth was touched by the request, but how would David react to the idea?

'Say yes. You've said that David wants to start healing this rift so it's the perfect opportunity.'

There was something in Maggie's voice, an eagerness which seemed out of all proportion. The quarrel was between David and Matthew. Why was it so important to Maggie also that the feud be ended? However, before Beth could question her, she heard the other woman's gasp of surprise.

'David! What are you doing here?'

'Business. Hello, Maggie...Beth. You never told me that you were coming into town today to meet Maggie.'

There was accusation in his deep voice and Beth flushed almost guiltily.

'She didn't tell you because she didn't know. We met by accident, didn't we, Beth?' If Maggie thought her reaction odd she hid it well, but Beth sensed a certain curiosity in the look the other woman gave her. Suddenly, it annoyed her intensely that David should have the temerity to speak to her in such a manner.

She met his eyes defiantly. 'That's right, but even if it hadn't been an accident I don't see why it should be a problem. I didn't realise that I had to give you a list of my comings and goings, David.'

His face tightened, his eyes boring into hers for a moment before the smoothly urbane mask slid into place. 'You'll have Maggie thinking I'm some sort of a tyrant, Beth, playing the heavy-handed husband.'

'I shall do no such thing! I'm sure you are just concerned about her. Isn't that right?' Maggie appeared blissfully unaware of the tension, but Beth wasn't. Temper rose inside her, hot and swift, and she glared angrily at him, but he ignored the look in a way that made her long to do something to shake that infuriating composure of his.

'Of course. I like to know where Beth is just in case there's a problem and she needs help.'

'I happen to be pregnant, not mentally deficient! If I need help then I am more than capable of finding it for myself!'

'I'm sure you are, but occasionally situations can arise when even you are glad to let someone else help you.' There was little inflexion in his voice, but Beth's face flamed. Since they had met, David had done nothing but help her, even to the point of marrying her, and suddenly, irrationally, she hated him for reminding her of the fact. She hit back unthinkingly in a way that she knew would shake him.

'Of course. Still, let's not quarrel about it now.' She gave a tinkly little laugh, seeing the way his eyes narrowed suspiciously, but he could never have foreseen what she was going to say in a million years. 'It doesn't seem appropriate right now, not when Maggie has just asked me to be Elizabeth's godmother. We don't want to give her the wrong impression by arguing, or she might change her mind!'

'I see. And do I take it that you have agreed?' There was no mistaking the anger now—she could hear it in his voice, sense it emanating from him, and her heart leapt with alarm, but she refused to back down.

'I was just about to when you arrived.' She turned back to Maggie with a strained little smile, surprised to see that the other woman seemed unaware of what had been going on. When had she, Beth, become so sensitive to David's every mood that she could tell how he was feeling? She had no idea, but it alarmed her that it should be so.

'Then that's settled. Thank you, Beth. I can't tell you how pleased I am.' Maggie hugged her, her face alight with pleasure as she looked from Beth to

David. 'I have to go now, but I'll ring you soon and let you know all the details. All right?'

Beth nodded, murmuring goodbye as she watched her leave the shop, then drew in a shaky little breath, all too aware of the silence. She shot a look sideways at David and felt her heart contract at the fury on his face.

'Damn you, woman, what gave you the right to start interfering in my life? Who gave you permission to meddle in things you know nothing at all about?'

'I . . . I'm your wife, David. Surely that gives me some rights?' Her voice shook, her whole body trembling as she held herself rigid against the bitter attack.

'Wife?' His grey eyes ran over her, cold as steel and filled with contempt. 'You're that all right and at this moment I wish with all my heart you weren't! Marrying you, Beth, must have been the biggest mistake I've ever made!'

He swung round on his heel and strode away, leaving her staring after him half blinded by tears. If he had made a mistake then so had she: a mistake agreeing to marry him, a mistake imagining for a moment that it could ever work out, a mistake letting herself believe that David Kane was the sort of warm, compassionate man she might come to love! Now all that was left was to rectify the mistakes as fast as she could.

The suitcase was heavy. Beth eased it off the bed then looked round the room to check she'd left nothing. It had taken longer to pack than she'd thought it would, her actions hampered by the stupid tears which kept blurring her vision. But now she was ready and there was no reason to linger.

She walked into the hall, straining against the weight of the case, then felt her heart lurch when she heard the sound of a key in the lock. She glanced wildly at her watch, desperately trying to reassure herself that it couldn't be David yet, but then the front door opened and he stepped inside.

He stopped when he saw her in the middle of the hall with the suitcase in her hand, his eyes taking in the scene with one swift, all-encompassing glance before his mouth curled derisively. 'You don't waste much time, do you, Beth? I must get you to do my packing next time I take a trip abroad. I could never have accomplished so much in such a short time!'

Her face flamed at the cold mockery and she looked away, desperate to avoid yet another confrontation, but it seemed it wasn't to be.

'Well, aren't you going to tell me where you're off to?' He looked round, feigning puzzlement. 'I can't see a note. Where did you leave it . . . in the sitting-room, or the study? Or didn't you bother to write me a note?' Suddenly the mockery disappeared to be replaced by a cold fury which made her take an involuntary step back.

'I . . . no. I didn't write you a note. I didn't see the need.'

'Didn't you? Not even for the sake of good manners? And I thought you were such a well-brought-up young woman. Yet you didn't see any reason to put pen to paper just to say thank you and goodbye?' He moved closer, his eyes like quicksilver in a face carved from stone. 'You were going to walk out of here and leave me guessing, weren't you?'

It was an effort to stand and face him, but she did. 'Yes!' She took a deep breath, feeling her chest aching from the pain as all the hurt welled up. 'You don't give a damn what happens to me, David Kane, so stop pretending. You made your feelings plain before, so plain that I don't owe you either thanks or explanations! Now please get out of my way. I have a taxi booked and I want to be downstairs when it arrives.'

'But I don't intend to get out of your way, Beth. What sort of husband would I be if I let you walk out like this?' He took the case from her hand and tossed it carelessly aside so that it hit the wall.

'Stop that! How dare you?' Beth went to push past him, but he caught her arms and held her.

'Oh, I dare all right. I dare do anything when you have the gall to plan on walking out without a word!' He shook her, not hard, not roughly, but with sufficient force to make her breath catch. 'Imagine how I would have felt if I'd come back and found you'd packed your things and left. Damn it, Beth! Don't you owe me anything at all?'

'Owe you?' She pulled away, rubbing her arms, but it was impossible to rub away the tingling imprint his fingers had left on her skin. 'I suppose I do owe you something. You've housed and fed me for some weeks now, haven't you? That must be worth quite a lot at London rates.' She pushed past him and walked over to the small table and pulled her cheque book from her bag. 'Let me write you a cheque to cover the costs. I'm afraid it won't be for the full amount as I'm a trifle low on funds right now. Maybe you can make up the shortfall by claiming the rest against your tax. I believe there is an allowance given for donations to charity, and that's what I've been for the last few weeks, isn't it, David? Your own personal charity case!'

She scribbled a cheque and handed it to him, her mouth set into a rigid smile to hide the pain. He accepted the paper and glanced at it, then slowly and deliberately tore it in half and let it drop to the floor.

'Are you deliberately trying to insult me, Beth?'

'Insult you? I was merely offering to pay for my keep. Lord knows you've gained little else from this arrangement so it's the least I can do. But if you won't accept payment then that's that. It just seems a shame that this "mistake" you made by asking me to marry you has cost you so much!'

'I was angry when I said that before. I won't apologise because you were in the wrong to start meddling in something you don't understand.'

'Understand? No, I don't understand any of it, David, and why? Because you don't want me to! But don't worry about it any more. It won't make any difference one way or another now. Goodbye.'

She swung round and wrenched the door open, hurrying through it towards the stairs, half blinded by tears.

'Beth!'

David shouted her name, his voice filled with such urgency that instinctively she glanced back over her shoulder just as she went to take the first step down. Her foot slipped on the edge of the tread and with a cry of fear she reached desperately for something to save herself, but there was nothing but space beneath her seeking hands. Pain knifed through her as she crashed against the metal handrail then rolled to the bottom of the stairs and lay in a crumpled heap. Seemingly in the distance a man was calling her name, repeating it over and over again with a desperation that vaguely surprised her, but then the darkness rose and claimed her and she heard nothing more.

CHAPTER SIX

THE hospital was quiet, the faint sounds of a trolley being wheeled along the corridor barely disturbing the silence in the small side room.

Beth lay in bed, her eyes closed, her face as white as the pillows. Her hands lay on her stomach, pressed lightly against the flatness, as she tried to come to terms with the knowledge that there would be no baby now. The doctors had been kind and patient as they'd quietly explained that everything possible had been done to save the child, but that in the end nature had taken its course. Now all she felt was a strange emptiness, as though part of her had been torn away. Somewhere during these few, too brief months she had come to love the child which had been such a shock when she'd first learned about it, but now she would never hold it in her arms, never touch it, care for it, watch it grow and learn to love her in return. If she could have cried then maybe it would have helped, but the grief she felt went deeper than tears.

The door opened and Beth looked round, forcing herself to return the nurse's smile.

'How are you feeling today, then, Mrs Kane?' She came over to the bed and took Beth's pulse, noting the figure down on the clip-chart hanging from the end of the bed.

'Much better, thank you, Nurse. My head doesn't ache quite so much.'

'Good. That's a sign that you're on the mend.' The nurse made another note on the chart then hung it back in its place. 'You might feel up to having a visitor, then?'

Beth looked away, feeling her stomach churning at the thought of who it might be. 'Who is it?'

'Your husband, of course. Look, Mrs Kane, I know you said that you didn't want to see him yet, but if you would just reconsider. The poor man is quite distraught. He's spent the last two days in the waiting-room, and I really think that——'

'No!' Beth interrupted her, her voice expressionless. 'I don't wish to see him just yet.'

'Very well. I suppose I shall have to tell him that.' There was disapproval on the nurse's face as she left the room, but Beth didn't care what she thought. She didn't want to see David yet, didn't want to remember that last ugly scene they'd had just before...

She closed her eyes, breathing slowly and deeply to combat the knifing pain in her chest at the memory of what had transpired between them. She couldn't cope with that now on top of the shock of losing the baby. It was too much to bear. Maybe later, when she felt strong emotionally, she would see him and speak to him without breaking down, but not right now.

'Beth.' His voice was low and soft, but she jumped as though he had shouted across the silence. The colour drained from her face as she looked towards the door and saw him standing just inside the room. Strain had etched deep lines into his face and shadowed his grey eyes with fatigue, but he looked so achingly familiar that she could have wept.

'Go away, David. I don't want to speak to you just now.'

'But I want to speak to you, Beth.' He let the door swing to, his face settling into lines of determination as he walked over to the bed and stared down at her. 'Why did you refuse to see me, Beth?'

Beth looked away, pulling herself up against the pillows before pushing her hair back with a shaking hand, feeling all the emotions just the sight of him aroused. This was what she'd been so desperate to avoid, this sharp, deep pain on top of the other pain about the loss of her baby, and now she wasn't sure if she could cope.

He swore softly, sitting down on the side of the bed to take her cold hand between both of his and smooth the trembling fingers. 'I'm sorry, Beth. I know it's not enough, but if I could turn back the clock and stop what happened then I would!'

There was such anguish in his deep voice that she turned at once to look at him. 'It was an accident, David. Just one of those horrible things that happen.' Tears shimmered in her eyes and she blinked to hold them at bay, more affected by his grief than she cared to admit.

'It didn't just happen. You were running away because of me! Because of all those cruel things I said to you. If I hadn't said what I did then the baby would . . .' He stood up abruptly and walked over to the window to stare out across the car park, his hands clenched into fists at his sides. 'There is no way I can ever make up to you what I've done, Beth. I don't blame you if you hate me.'

'I don't hate you, David. I...' She broke off, wondering what to say, how to tell him that hate was the very last emotion she could ever feel for him. It hadn't been hatred that had made her pack her bags and run that day, but fear of the hurt he could inflict on her. She'd been hurt so badly by Andrew's betrayal, but if she was honest then she had to face the fact that what David had said about their marriage being a mistake had hurt her far more.

'What? Tell me, Beth. We have to clear this up once and for all.' He swung round to face her, straightening as though ready to face any objections she might make. 'Maybe I am being unreasonable at present in view of what's happened, but I'm not prepared to let this go on festering. I want it sorted out here and now.'

She shook her head. 'Nothing. It doesn't matter now. It's better that we forget all about what's gone on. Once I'm on my feet again I'll collect my things and then you can put me and everything that's happened out of your mind.'

'I have no intention of doing that.' He came back to the bed, his face stern and uncompromising as he stared harshly down at her. 'Are you trying to tell me that you still intend to leave me, Beth?'

'Naturally. It was what I was doing that day...' She broke off, swallowing hard, then drew in a breath as she fought for control. 'You said yourself that this marriage was a mistake, David. Let's end it here and now and be done with the whole farce. After all, the main reason why you married me no longer exists.' Her hand smoothed over her stomach in an unconscious little gesture and she looked away, missing the pain which crossed his face.

'You're right—there is no longer the baby to think about—but as for you implying that our marriage is unnecessary now...That's not quite so, Beth.'

'What do you mean?' Her head came up as she searched his face for any clue to what he meant, but there was nothing she could read in his expression.

'I've been talking to the doctor and he says that you are going to need a few months to get back on your feet again. How do you intend to manage if you leave when you have no place to live and no means of supporting yourself?'

'I'll manage somehow! I don't need your charity any longer, David!'

'It was never charity, Beth, and you know that. Don't be a fool. You know yourself that you'll need time to recover both physically and mentally from losing the baby. I want you to come back to the flat when the doctor pronounces you well enough to go home, and I don't want to hear any more silly talk of ending this marriage just now.'

'You don't want? And how about what I want for a change?' She glared back at him. 'You made your feelings very plain the other day, David, and I'll be damned if I'll go back where I'm not wanted!'

'But I do want you, Beth.' His voice was suddenly soft and low, so vibrant with emotion that Beth felt her senses flare. Just for a moment she let her eyes linger on his handsome face before deliberately looking away to break the spell those deep tones had cast over her.

'You don't mean that, David,' she said quietly. 'I'm just an inconvenience to you and always have been.'

He laughed softly, tilting her face with gentle fingers to stare straight into her eyes. 'You have never been an inconvenience, Beth. Never. I was angry that day, too angry to think about what I was saying.'

'You said what you meant. Maybe I deserved it in a way.' She smiled sadly. 'I never meant to interfere in your life. I just wanted to hit back at you for reminding me how much I owed you. I shall phone Maggie and explain once I leave here.'

He shook his head, his eyes lingering on her face in a way that made the blood swirl along her veins. 'Don't worry about that. All I want is for you to get better, Beth. That's my primary concern and you won't do that if you insist on trying to fend for yourself while you're still so weak.' Slowly, gently, he bent and kissed her lips, his mouth lingering for a mere heartbeat before he straightened. 'I want you to come back to the flat, Beth, at least until you're well enough to make any fresh plans. But there's no rush. I can't ever make up to you what you've lost, but I can at least make sure that you are cared for until you're better. So promise me that you'll do that, eh?'

Beth nodded, every objection melted by the stunning warmth of that brief kiss. When he stood up she stared silently up at him, unaware that the shock showed in her eyes. He smiled almost gently, reaching out to touch her chcek in a brief caress.

'I'd better go before that nurse discovers me in here against her orders. But I shall be back to see you tonight, Beth.'

He left and Beth lay weakly back against the pillows, her head swirling with emotions. She wanted to believe what that sweet, gentle kiss seemed to imply, but in the depths of her mind a small voice was whispering a warning she had to heed. David had told her why he didn't want to end this marriage of theirs yet, but had he been entirely truthful? He had touched upon the fact that she would need support over the coming months, but never once had he mentioned the feud with his brother. That had been a deciding factor in his asking her to marry him in the first place and she couldn't afford to forget its importance now. If she stayed then she had always to remember that David had reasons for helping her that he had never fully explained. It would be foolish to ever let herself forget about them and be swayed purely by emotion.

Beth had been home from hospital for over a fortnight when Maggie telephoned. She'd spent the morning wandering aimlessly around the flat, wishing that David would leave her some work to do. He'd been adamant about not letting her touch any of the letters since she'd got back, insisting that she spend the time resting to recover her strength. However, Beth was determined to make him see sense soon. Time hung heavy on her hands with so little to do apart from make the odd meal, giving her too much time to brood. She wanted to be kept busy to stop the painful thoughts about the baby from filling her mind all the time. Now the sound of the phone ringing was a welcome diversion.

'Beth? How are you feeling? It's Maggie.'

'Much better, thanks. And you?'

'Oh, not too bad considering the fact that Elizabeth had me awake most . . . Oh, Beth, I'm sorry! I didn't mean to say that of all things.'

'Don't be silly, Maggie. It's something I have to come to terms with. I can't expect other people not to talk about their children just because I've lost the baby.' The sorrow ran deep in her voice and she heard Maggie sigh softly.

'It must be hard, Beth. I can only try to imagine what you're going through. I wish I could help, do something to ease the pain for both you and David.'

'You can help by acting as naturally as possible. I don't want you to think you mustn't mention Elizabeth. It hurts, of course, but I have to face it.'

'You are brave, Beth. I'm sure I would never be able to cope the way you have. David was saying the other day how marvellous you've been.'

'Oh, you've seen him, then?' There was no reason why a *frisson* of unease should run along her veins, but it did. Beth clutched the receiver tighter, feeling tension curling inside her as she waited to hear what Maggie would say.

'Just fleetingly. I ran into him when I was out shopping the other day, much the same way as we did when we had coffee. Didn't he mention that he had seen me?'

'No. He must have forgotten, I expect.'

'Probably. He was in rather a hurry at the time and only stopped for a moment to tell me what had happened.'

'I see.'

'I wish I'd known sooner, Beth. I could have come to see you in the hospital, although you probably didn't feel much like having visitors, apart from David. At least you have each other to fall back on, and I know for a fact that David is a person you can depend on completely in a time of stress.'

She sounded so certain that somehow it surprised Beth. Maggie and David treated each other with a cool civility when they met, yet there had been something in her voice just then which told Beth that she knew David far better than that implied. Had they been close friends once but had to break off that friendship because of the feud? It would explain the rather stilted way they treated one another. Naturally Maggie would always feel that her loyalties must lie first and foremost with her husband.

The tension eased from her, making her respond more naturally to the statement. 'He certainly is. From the word go I've found myself relying on him, probably more than I should in the circumstances.'

'What circumstances?' Maggie laughed. 'That sounds very mysterious, Beth.'

'Does it?' Beth forced a laugh, inwardly cursing herself for the unconscious slip. 'I didn't mean it to.' Hurriedly she changed the subject. 'You must come round some time, Maggie. I'll make us both some lunch and then we can have a proper chat.'

'I'd love that. Actually, in a way that was one of the reasons why I was phoning you today. Look, Beth, tell me no if you don't want to go through with it, because I'll understand.'

'Go through with what? Now who's being mysterious?'

'Standing as Elizabeth's godmother. The christening is only a week away now and unfortunately I can't put it back because there are people coming from all over the place. It's too late now to make fresh plans. I still want you to stand for her, but I shall understand if you feel you can't do it.'

Beth took a slow painful breath, her face clouding over. It would be painful, poignantly so in view of her recent loss. Could she handle it?

'I've spoken to Matthew about it, Beth, and he's just as keen as I am that you go through with it as long as you feel up to it.'

'Is he? Then he must have a markedly different view from David's.' Her voice was sharper than she'd intended and Maggie was silent for a moment before she said quietly,

'Was David very annoyed that day when we met in town? It never occurred to me that he might be until later when I got to thinking about what had gone on. I did wonder if I'd put my foot in it.'

What could she say? Since she'd come back from hospital David had made no further mention of what had caused that bitter row between them. Beth had the feeling that he was determined to bury it once and for all, so would it be wise to rake it all up again? 'Of course you didn't. Don't be silly. I'd love to say yes, Maggie, but . . .' She tailed off, torn between loyalty to David and a desire not to go back on a promise.

'But you're not sure how David feels. Oh, Beth, I'd give anything to end this stupid quarrel, any single thing under the sun! Matthew has got as far as stating that it's time it was all sorted out, but that's it. He's too damned stubborn to take the next step and meet David and talk!'

'What caused the row between them, Maggie? I don't mean to pry, but I need to know.' She laughed almost bitterly. 'Sometimes it seems to me that everything hinges on it.'

'I really don't feel that I can explain it to you, Beth. David is the one who should do that.' Maggie was obviously distressed at being questioned and Beth bit back an impatient sigh. The trouble was that she'd had too much time to brood recently, and this quarrel between David and his brother had started to take on a greater and greater importance the more she thought about it.

'I'm sorry. Forget I said anything. As for the christening, well, I would love to say yes here and now, but I think I should talk to David first and see how he feels.'

'Of course. I don't want to be the cause of any trouble between you. Give me a ring as soon as you can to let me know. I hope it's yes because I can't think of anyone I would rather have as Elizabeth's godmother.'

The warmth in Maggie's voice was genuine and Beth felt comforted by it. She had the feeling that they could become good friends if circumstance allowed. After getting all the details of where and when the ceremony was to take place she hung up and spent the day buoyed up by the pleasant exchange. However, when she heard the front door opening she was suddenly assailed by doubts as to the wisdom of what she was doing. Was it really sensible to risk disturbing the harmony that they had maintained since she'd left hospital by pursuing a course of action that David seemed opposed to? He would think that she was trying to interfere in his life again, and the memory of what had happened the last time was still too fresh in her mind.

'What's the matter, Beth?' Obviously sensing her disturbed state of mind, he stopped beside her chair, staring intently down at her, but Beth refused to meet his eyes as all her doubts rose up. She didn't want to force his hand and start a confrontation again. She didn't want to put herself in a position whereby he might tell her to leave, because the thought of never seeing him again was too much to bear.

'For heaven's sake, Beth, what is it? Don't you feel well? Answer me.'

It was impossible to ignore his mounting impatience. 'I'm fine, David.'

'Then tell me what's been going on.' He towered over her, big and dangerous-looking in his dark suit and white shirt with his grey eyes glittering in the light cast by the lamp. They had been married for weeks now, but when he stood there glaring at her she felt she hardly knew him at all.

Something of what she felt must have shown on her face because he turned away abruptly and dropped down into a chair. 'Just tell me what's wrong. I won't bite your head off, so stop looking as though I scare you half to death.'

Beth took a deep breath, realising with a pang that she was going about things all the wrong way. 'You don't scare me, David. It's just that . . . that I don't know how you're going to react to what I have to ask you.'

His face tightened, but his voice remained cool and level. 'Then maybe you'd better tell me what it is.'

'Maggie phoned today. She asked me again if I would be Elizabeth's godmother.'

The words hung in the air, bare and unadorned, and Beth held her breath as she waited to see if the storm would break over her head again as it had done before. However David's voice held little but bland acceptance when he spoke.

'And what did you tell her?'

'That I would ask you first.' She stared back at him, colour ebbing and flowing in her face. 'I don't want to start another row, David, by interfering. Just tell me how you feel about the idea.'

'How I feel?' His tone was harshly bitter, sending a chill coursing through her, and she closed her eyes in despair. She couldn't bear it if it happened again, if he reiterated what he'd said that day. Their marriage might have been forged for any number of strange reasons, but Beth was honest enough to admit that it was the most important thing she had left in her life. It was the one good thing she had to cling to, her mainstay in a world which had been turned upside-down over the past few months.

She opened her eyes to tell him to forget all about the idea, then stopped abruptly when she saw that he had got up to stand by the window. The night had drawn in so that the glass took on the appearance of a darkened mirror, throwing David's reflection back into the room. Beth sat quite still, watching the fleeting emotions which crossed his face. Pain, regret and a deep, deep sorrow all showed so sharply that she felt like an intruder witnessing so many private emotions, but when he turned back to look at her the mask was once more back in place.

'If you want to be the child's godmother then that's up to you, Beth. It's your decision to make.'

'But is it what you want?' Suddenly she knew she had to be sure how he felt.

He smiled faintly, his mouth curving upwards, yet his eyes remained strangely blank. 'Maybe it isn't a question of what I want any longer, but more a question of what is right.'

'You're talking about the quarrel with your brother. Maggie wouldn't tell me anything about it. She said I must ask you.'

'Perhaps I will tell you one day, Beth. But not right now. Let's take it all one step at a time, shall we? When is this christening to be?'

He wouldn't tell her. Beth felt a deep regret she could barely hide at his refusal to share the secret with her. 'A week's time, at the church in the village where you and Matthew used to live. Evidently they are staying at your old home until the tenants who rented their house leave. Maggie has asked if we'll go down and stay for the weekend, but that's up to you. If you'd prefer not to do that, it's fine by me.'

'Why not?' He smiled harshly, his grey eyes betraying nothing of what he was really feeling. Beth experienced the most ridiculous urge to do something to shake him, to make him tell her what he was thinking, but that was something she wouldn't do again, not after the last disastrous time.

'Are you sure? We can just go on the Sunday if it would make things easier?'

'Stop worrying about it. I've agreed to go, so leave it at that.'

'How can I when I don't know how you really feel? I'm worried about you getting hurt, David!' The words came out before she could stop them and he stilled at once, searching her face. Then slowly he came towards her and took her hands to draw her to her feet and hold her close in his arms, so close that she could feel the heavy thud of his heart against her breast, feel the long, strong line of his thighs against her own. She closed her eyes, leaning against him, shaken to the core by the wild surge of sensation which shot through her at his touch.

He set her from him, his hands resting at the back of her waist as he stared down into her face. 'Have you ever wondered what it would be like if we changed the rules a bit?'

Her breath felt tight, her heart pounding. It was the way he was looking at her: he had never looked at her like that before, looked at her the way a man looks at a woman he wants.

'I . . . I don't know what you mean.'

Her voice was a husky whisper and he smiled gently. 'The rules of this marriage of ours. Have you never wondered what it would be like if it wasn't just a sham, but real?'

'No.' It was a lie and she knew at once that he understood that, and flushed wildly.

'No?'

She didn't know if she liked being teased this way and pushed against his chest, but he refused to let her go. She glared up at him, all too aware that her heart was beating like a drum and even more conscious that he must be able to feel it. 'What's got into you, David? Is this some sort of a game? Because if it is then I don't like it!'

'It isn't a game. I'm quite serious. What is to stop us from making this marriage into a real one?'

'What's to stop us?' Bitterness welled inside her. 'Have you forgotten already why you married me? I might have lost the baby, David, but that was the reason why it came about in the first place, and I haven't forgotten that even if you have!'

'I haven't forgotten anything. Not the baby or Andrew.' He let her go abruptly and walked over to the desk to pick up a silver paper-knife. 'However, you can't spend the rest of your life pining for what might have been. We could have a good life together, Beth. We could even have a child of our own if you wanted.'

It was pure temptation and her heart bled as she struggled to find the words to dismiss the idea while she still had the strength. 'But you don't love me! You know you don't!'

He shrugged, setting the knife down with a clatter which made her flinch. 'That is irrelevant. Love isn't the be-all and end-all of a relationship.'

Irrelevant? It was everything. Now, more than ever, she knew that. Being here with David, living with him day by day, was slowly teaching her that, although she shied away from wondering why.

'I don't know what to say to convince you how ridiculous the idea is, David.'

'Then don't try. Just think about it, then maybe you'll see that it makes sense.'

'Sense?' She laughed almost hysterically. 'I don't know what makes sense any more!'

'That's because you're confused. You've been through a lot recently, Beth. You need time to think things through.' He came back and took her face between his hands to tilt it to his. 'I could give you another child, Beth, if that's what you want, but I don't intend to rush you into making a decision you might come to regret.'

He brushed her mouth with his, his lips so tender, so gentle that she barely had time to feel the kiss before he let her go. 'Think about it, Beth. That's all I ask.'

She touched her mouth, feeling the lingering whisper of heat his lips had left behind, a heat which stayed tantalisingly with her for the rest of the night so that when she lay in bed it wasn't the rights or wrongs of turning their marriage into a real one which she thought about, but how wonderful it would be to have David kiss her like that all the time.

CHAPTER SEVEN

BETH had taken great care with her appearance, brushing her red-gold hair until it shimmered like shot silk as it curled on to the shoulders of her navy wool dress, but as she looked in the mirror she experienced a deep, very feminine regret that her figure still hadn't regained its usual slender lines.

Picking up the delicate cameo brooch that had been her mother's, she pinned it to the shoulder of the dress, but it did little in her eyes to detract from the rich curves of her body. With a rare show of temper, she snatched up her hairbrush and flung it across the room, then jumped guiltily when the telephone suddenly rang.

There was a snap in her voice when she picked up the receiver, a bite which just about covered the threatening tears. Her emotions still seemed to swing from one extreme to the other, laughter turning to tears almost at the touch of a button. Perhaps it was still the lingering shock of the miscarriage or maybe it was the tension which seemed to fill the flat whenever she and David were together now. She didn't know which it was, but her nerves were raw from living like this.

'Yes?'

'Mmm, you don't sound too pleased with life. What's the matter, Beth? Has something upset you?'

FREE books and gifts claim

Yes! Please send me four Temptations and two FREE gifts without obligation. Please also reserve me a subscription to Reader Service; which means that I can look forward to four brand new Temptations for just £7.40 each month (subject to VAT). Postage and packing is FREE. If I decide not to subscribe I will write to you within 10 days. Any free books and gifts will remain mine to keep. I understand that I may cancel or suspend my subscription at any time. I am over 18 years of age.

7A3T

Ms/Mrs/Miss/Mr ______________________________

Address ______________________________

____

______________________ **Postcode** ____________

Signature ______________________________

NO STAMP NEEDED

Mills & Boon
Reader Service
FREEPOST
P.O. Box 236
Croydon
CR9 9EL

Colour flooded her face as she heard David's deep tones and she took a quick little breath to stem the wild leap her heart gave. It kept happening all the time now since that day he'd kissed her and asked her to think about making their marriage real and, although he had never mentioned the subject again, Beth knew it lay between them like an almost tangible presence.

'There's nothing wrong. Why should there be? What have you rung for? Are you going to be late?'

'I'm afraid so.' His tone was cool, smooth, untroubled by all the tension which affected her, it seemed. How she envied him that composure, that ability to hide his feelings. She had the idea that he knew exactly how she'd been feeling recently and the reasons for it. It wasn't a comforting thought at all. David was far too clever and astute to miss an opportunity to get what he wanted, but Beth didn't want to be rushed into making any decision she might regret.

'What time will you get here, then?'

'I won't. I've been expecting a special delivery, but so far it hasn't materialised. I can't take a chance on missing it so I'll get one of the men to collect you in my car. I take it that you're all ready and packed?'

Beth bit back a sigh, all too conscious of the edge in his voice now. They were due at Maggie's in a few hours' time and she still wasn't certain that it was the right thing to do. 'Yes. Everything is ready.'

'Good. I'll tell Bill to come up to the flat for the bags. He should be there in half an hour or so, depending on the traffic.'

'All right. David . . . well, you are sure that it's what you want, aren't you? It isn't too late to ring Maggie and tell her we won't be coming.'

'And have my dear brother thinking that I can't face him? I don't think so, Beth!'

He rang off abruptly and Beth replaced the receiver, wishing that she'd left well alone. That was part of the trouble: she was becoming far too involved in David's affairs, starting to care too deeply how he felt. As she recovered her strength she should be starting to make plans for the future, starting to work out where her life was going, but it seemed impossible to separate her life from his, to imagine a future which didn't have him as the focal point. It would be so easy to let herself fall in love with David, so easy yet so dangerous because he would never love her in return, and she couldn't face the thought of being hurt again.

The factory was quiet when she arrived. Beth thanked the driver then made her way in through the door he indicated, looking round the huge room with surprise. When she'd imagined the factory, she'd expected to see rows of gleaming machinery turning out various items of furniture, but that wasn't the case at all.

Slowly she made her way down the long room, studying the tools laid out on the workbenches, craftsmen's tools used for making furniture by hand in the traditional way. She came to the end of the bench and stopped, unable to resist drawing a sheet aside to examine the chest of drawers it was covering, and gasped in delight at the elegant lines, the workmanship which carried the hallmark of centuries of skill.

'Like it?' David suddenly appeared at her side, smiling at the stunned admiration on her face.

'Of course! It's gorgeous.' She looked round, skimming a glance over other pieces all shrouded against the dust. 'I had no idea you made furniture like this, despite all those letters I've typed for you!'

He laughed deeply, leaning back against the bench while he watched her with amused eyes. 'What did you imagine? Mass-produced stuff churned out in its dozens?' He shook his head, his blond hair gleaming in the soft half-light. 'I'm not interested in that. I make individual items here, collectors' pieces made by craftsmen who have spent years learning their trade. The mass market holds no appeal whatsoever.'

'I can understand why.' She stroked her fingers over the chest then let the cover drop back into place. 'But who buys furniture like this? It must be dreadfully expensive.'

'Quality costs, whatever it is you're buying. However, lack of orders isn't a problem. The business has gone from strength to strength since I started it. The order books are full for the next three years, in fact.'

'You must have found your place in the market, then.'

'I have, fortunately. It was a gamble, I'll admit that, but I started small, just me making the first few items, and have gone on from there. I now employ twelve men and am looking towards taking on a couple more in the next few months if I can find any skilled enough for the work we do here.'

'You? You made the furniture yourself?'

'I did. I still do, in fact. That's one of the reasons

why I have so much paperwork to do when I'm at home. I spend as much time as is feasible working with my hands.' He laughed mockingly, taking her arm to lead her across the room. 'I can see you're not wholly convinced. Take a look at this. I had been intending to keep it as a surprise until it was completely finished, but as you're here you may as well see it now.'

He drew a cover aside, watching her expression as she stared down at the exquisite work-box with its lid inlaid with a delicate pattern of roses and lily of the valley surrounding a flowing letter 'B'.

'For me?'

'Of course. It has your initial on it, doesn't it, Beth? I wanted to make you something special, Beth. To try to make up for everything you've been through recently. Something beautiful to keep.'

'Oh, David! I don't know what to say.' She turned to him, her eyes glistening with tears as she went on tiptoe to kiss him quickly on the cheek. He steadied her, his hands warm and strong against her waist as he looked down into her face, and Beth felt her pulse leap at his expression.

'You don't always need words to say what you mean, Beth. There are other ways.' Slowly, so slowly, he bent and touched his mouth to hers, his lips warm and tender at first before they became more demanding. Beth shuddered, feeling the hot, swift surge of desire flowing along her veins. For the past few days she had guarded the memory of that other kiss, but even that hadn't prepared her for this heady, demanding assault on her senses. Last time the kiss had been a sweet promise of things that could be, but this was so very different.

This time David wasn't giving, he was demanding, wasn't promising, but taking. He kissed her now as a man kissed a woman he intended to arouse, to master, to take with him to some private place where no one else could intrude, and suddenly Beth knew that whatever David wanted from her she would give.

Her hands came up to slide inside his jacket and across the warm, hard muscles of his chest while her lips parted to admit the entry of his tongue, and everything seemed to flare out of control as he realised that she wasn't going to resist. He drew her closer, his hand burrowing under the silky length of her hair to hold her head while he deepened the kiss until she moaned in ecstasy at the hot swirl of sensations which flooded her. When his hand slid down the smooth column of her neck then moved on to cover her breast she arched towards him, gasping as she felt his fingers brushing and teasing her hardening nipple to life.

'Beth.' Her name was hot and sweet as he said it that way in that slow, deep voice and she shuddered convulsively, clinging to him as her legs went weak. He supported her against the long line of his powerful body, his mouth skimming up her cheek to press kisses to the corner of her eye, her forehead, then down the straight line of her nose until his lips just brushed the top of hers and then stopped tantalisingly out of reach.

'David . . . please.' She was barely aware of what she was saying, barely aware that her voice held a plea in its soft tones, but he heard it.

'Please what, Beth?' His lips brushed hers, softly, gently, making her ache for a deeper contact, and she turned to capture his mouth, but once again he eluded her.

'Tell me, Beth. Tell me what you want.' His voice was smooth as satin, soft as silk, deep as velvet, and she shivered in response.

'Kiss me, David . . . please.'

There was a moment when he seemed to hesitate, but then she felt his mouth take hers while he kissed her with a passion which left her clinging helplessly to him. She had never felt this way before, never felt the blood surge along her veins like fire, never felt the beat of her heart in every cell, never felt as though one kiss held the whole world. Never! Not even when Andrew had kissed her.

The thought came from nowhere, sharp and bitterly painful, shattering the magic with devastating speed. She pulled away, her face pale, her eyes haunted. She'd thought she'd loved Andrew, the father of her lost child, but the touch of David's mouth had made a mockery out of that. Shame swept over her, hot and heavy, and she turned away, hating herself for her blind stupidity, hating David for making her admit the truth at last: what she'd felt for Andrew had never been love!

'There's nothing to feel ashamed about, Beth. Physical desire between a man and a woman is the most natural thing in the world.'

'Is it?' She spun round, her hands clenched into fists as she strove for control. 'I'm afraid that is something I have little experience of despite the evidence to the contrary. I know little about the opposite sex and how natural desire can be! It might surprise you to learn that Andrew was the first and only man I have ever slept with, and that was hardly a success!'

She regretted the revealing statement the very instant she saw the way his eyes narrowed. From the first moment they had met, Andrew had tried to talk her into bed with him, but when she had finally agreed she knew that he had found it a disappointing experience. His remarks had been scathing at the time and Beth had been bitterly hurt, attributing his disappointment to her own shortcomings. She had hated the whole experience if she was truthful, which made it all the more worrying how she'd just responded to David.

'That doesn't surprise me, Beth, although I do wonder what he was doing wrong if you found it so unsatisfactory.' He skimmed a glance over her face, his eyes lingering on the bruised softness of her lips before looking straight into her eyes. 'You are a very sensual woman, Beth. A man would have to be completely insensitive to your needs not to find that out. But there again, maybe you only respond that way with the right man?'

What did he mean? That he was the right man to teach her how to respond? Beth fought against the idea, but it only served to strengthen her own shocked feelings. David had seemingly only to touch her, kiss her, and she became a different woman in his arms from the one who had suffered Andrew's lovemaking as a duty rather than a pleasure.

'I...no! No, you're wrong. You...you caught me at a moment of weakness, that's all.' There was more desperation than conviction in her voice, and he smiled harshly.

'Is that right? Maybe we should test it out, see if what we just enjoyed was a fluke?' He reached for her, intent written all over his arrogant face, but Beth knocked his hands away.

'No! Stop it, David. I don't want to test anything out. I know how I feel.' She laughed suddenly, struck by an unpalatable thought. 'Was that what it was all in aid of, some sort of a test to see how I would respond?'

His eyes glittered and he straightened so that he seemed to tower over her. 'I kissed you because I wanted to, Beth. I wanted to feel your mouth under mine, sweet and responsive, and I'll be damned if I'll lie and say differently! You might be able to lie to yourself about your feelings, but I felt how you responded just now and you were with me . . . with *me* . . . all the way!'

How could she deny it? How could she turn something magical and beautiful into a tissue of lies? She turned away, her head bowed so that she wouldn't have to look at him. 'I'll wait in the car for you.'

'All right. We'll let it drop for now if that's what you want. But some day soon you're going to have to face up to how you feel.'

She swung round, her hair flying about her face in a silken cloud of rich gold. 'Maybe, but leave me to worry about that. You have your own ghosts to lay this weekend, David, so why not concentrate your energies on doing that?'

He stared at her for a moment that seemed to stretch to infinity. 'Maybe I've already laid my ghosts to rest, Beth.'

What did he mean? Why should those few quiet words make hope flood through her body? She'd tried once before to build a future on dreams and she knew how dangerous and foolish it could be. Now all she wanted was to rebuild her life on rock-solid certainties.

The house was set at the end of a long gravelled driveway. Beth sat and studied it in silence as David turned the car in through the gates. They'd said little on the drive from town, keeping conversation to a minimum, and Beth could feel her head starting to throb from the tension. The sight of the forbidding red-brick house didn't ease that tension one little bit.

David stopped the engine then sat staring at the house, his expression guarded. What was he thinking about—what had happened in the factory, or the coming meeting with his brother? Whatever it was, Beth felt the sudden need to reassure him.

'It will be fine, David; I know it will.'

He looked almost blankly at her for a moment then turned to open the car door. 'I'm sure it will. Shall we go in?'

The cool rebuff hurt, but she refused to show it as she unfastened her seatbelt and followed him from the car. He took her arm and guided her up the steep steps, but before he could ring the bell the front door was flung open and Maggie appeared.

'Hello! I was just starting to get worried. You're later than I expected you to be.'

Beth forced a warm smile, walking ahead of David into the hall. 'Sorry. David had to wait for a delivery so we set off rather later than planned. I hope it hasn't put you out at all?'

'Of course not.' She gave Beth a swift hug then looked past her, the smile fading slightly. 'How are you, David? I'm so glad that you could come.'

David came further into the hall and closed the door. 'You have Beth to thank for that. She can be very persuasive when she sets her mind to it.'

Maggie gave a tremulous little smile, her green eyes clouding when she heard the hard note in his deep voice. 'Then Matthew and I are doubly grateful to her. I shall . . .' She broke off abruptly, her whole body tensing as footsteps echoed along the hall. Beth looked past her, studying the man who had come into the hall. He was as tall as David, with the same wide shoulders and leanly muscled physique, but there the similarity ended. Matthew Kane was as dark as David was fair, his black hair gleaming in the muted light from the chandelier, his dark eyes unreadable in his set face. He looked dark and forbidding as he stood there and unconsciously Beth moved closer to David.

He immediately sensed her unease, glancing quickly at her pale face before he slid an arm around her shoulders and drew her closer. 'Matthew. You're looking fit.'

Matthew nodded, his eyes skimming from his brother to Beth and back again. 'So are you. I was sorry to hear about your recent loss. Maggie told me about the baby and you have my sympathies.'

'Thank you.' The reply was curt almost to the point of rudeness and Beth shivered convulsively, feeling the tension filling the hall. What had gone on in the past was still vividly alive and she'd been a fool to think that anything could change it easily.

Maggie obviously felt the same way because her smile was forced when she looked from one to the other. 'Why don't we all go inside and have a drink? You two must be dying for something after driving all this way.'

David shook his head, his fingers gripping Beth's shoulder in a silent warning not to disagree. 'No, thanks. I think it would be better if we unpacked our things first. Beth must be tired so, if you don't mind, I'm sure she would like some time to rest before dinner.'

'Of course not. I should have thought about that before.' She turned to Matthew, her face softening. 'Darling, would you mind helping David with the cases? I'll just take Beth up and show her where everything is.'

Matthew looked back at his wife, the harshness leaving his face for a moment, and Beth felt her breath catch at the expression of love in his eyes. 'No, of course not. You go on ahead and leave them to us.'

Maggie reached up and kissed him swiftly on the cheek then turned back to Beth, her smile less strained now. 'Ready, Beth? I've put you in one of the rooms which overlook the garden at the back. It's rather a gloomy-looking room at night when there's only electric light to brighten it, but in the morning if the sun is shining it's rather charming.'

Beth smiled back, doing her best to follow Maggie's lead and ease the tension. 'I'm sure it will be lovely, Maggie. Thank you.'

She followed Maggie up the stairs and along the landing, pausing in the doorway to look round the room. As Maggie had said, it was rather a gloomy room with its heavy Victorian furniture and stiff burgundy-red drapes, but the high windows would let in a lot of light during the daytime.

Maggie glanced round the room and grimaced. 'It's definitely not to my taste, but the whole house hasn't been altered in years. It was Matthew's grandparents' house and when his father married he took it over and they lived here. Not that either Matthew or David were here that much. They were both packed off to school at a very early age, but it can't have been a comfortable place to live. Nobody could call it homely!'

Beth laughed, dropping her bag on to the bed before kicking off her shoes. 'I take it that you aren't intending to make your home here permanently, then?'

'No way! We're only staying until the tenants vacate our house in town. Quite apart from the fact that I find it utterly depressing, it's too far out of the city. Matthew would never be able to travel into work each day and there is no way I am having him living in town on his own and coming back here just for weekends. That isn't my idea of marriage, although Matthew's parents lived like that.'

'Is his father still practising law? David has mentioned his mother, but never said anything about his father.' She asked the question almost idly, then flushed when she saw Maggie's surprise. The trouble was that she knew so little about David's background, but she would have to be more careful about admitting it or it would give rise to speculation.

'His father died a couple of years ago and his mother now lives on the coast. You'll meet her on Sunday at the christening. I take it that you haven't met her yet?'

Beth avoided Maggie's eyes as she stood up and carried her vanity case over to the dressing-table and started to unpack her toiletries. 'Not yet.'

'Beth, maybe I shouldn't ask this, but everything is all right between you and David, isn't it?'

'Of course. Why do you ask?' She tried to inject amusement into her tone, but Maggie seemed less than convinced.

'There's just something... I don't know how to describe it, but you two don't act like a married couple.'

'Maybe we haven't had enough practice at it as yet.' David spoke from the doorway, making them both jump. He carried the rest of the cases into the room, glancing quickly from one to the other, and Beth felt a ridiculous rush of heat flow along her veins. Colour ran up her cheeks and she turned away, but not fast enough to hide it from Maggie's discerning eyes.

'That's probably it, especially when you can still make Beth blush like that.'

'That is one of her most endearing habits.' His voice was soft and filled with something that made Beth's heart leap. She looked round, feeling the heat of desire flowing along her limbs. Time seemed to stand still, locking them into a single precious moment, then Maggie spoke and the spell was broken.

'I'll leave you to get settled in. Dinner is at eight.'

She left the room, but it was several minutes before Beth could get herself back under control to speak. 'I'd better unpack.' She glanced at the two cases standing beside the bed and frowned. 'You've brought your case in here by mistake, David. Hadn't you better take it to your room and start unpacking?'

'This is my room. Naturally Maggie assumed that we would be sharing a bedroom. Most married couples do.'

'Share? Oh, but...' She tailed off, her heart thundering as she realised what he'd said was right. Obviously Maggie would expect them to share a bedroom. Why hadn't she thought about it before?

'We're both adults, Beth. I'm sure we can manage for a couple of nights. After all, you were the one who wanted to come.'

That was so unfair that she rounded on him. 'You agreed! You said that it was time to end this stupid quarrel with your brother. Don't try making it out to be my fault.'

'I wasn't. I was merely pointing out that if the idea of sharing a bed with me is so abhorrent then you should have thought about it sooner.' His eyes were like ice as he skimmed a contemptuous look over her. 'Don't worry, Beth. You will be quite safe. I shall manage to curb any lustful thoughts I may have!'

He strode out of the room, leaving Beth shaking with a strange mixture of emotions. Anger, fear and a strange sense of hurt at that parting shot. Did he have to make it seem that the last thing he would ever feel for her was desire? He'd seemed ready enough to admit that he could want her back in the factory, but had that been, as she'd accused him, some sort of a test?

She walked back to the bed and opened her case, forcing herself to concentrate as she stowed the contents neatly away, but it was impossible to cut David out of her thoughts, just as it was impossible to work out exactly what it was he wanted from her.

CHAPTER EIGHT

BETH'S eyelids felt heavy, weighted down by sleep. She rolled over on to her side, burrowing her face deeper into the pillow to blot out the light that was waking her up, but it didn't work. She blinked sleepily, rubbing her eyes to clear her vision, then felt every sense flare to life when she saw the figure standing in a patch of sunlight streaming through the window.

Naked apart from a towel wound around his narrow hips, the man's body gleamed hard and golden in the pale morning light, droplets of water sparkling against the smooth perfection of muscle and sinew. He looked like some beautifully carved statue as he stood there, but then he suddenly turned and Beth felt her breath catch when she recognised David.

'So you're awake at last. I was wondering if you were going to sleep the clock round.' He came across to the bed and looked down at her, his grey eyes warm, his mouth curved into a tender little smile, and Beth felt a slow ripple of heat curl along her veins. She looked away, running the tip of her tongue over her dry lips, totally disorientated. She remembered unpacking her clothes, remembered taking off the navy dress and hanging it away before lying down on the bed to rest for a few minutes, but after that she remembered nothing apart from some hazy, disturbing dreams. Had she really been asleep since then?

The mattress dipped as David sat down on the side of the bed and Beth swung round to face him, feeling her heart leap treacherously at his nearness. Just for a moment she met his eyes, then looked away, unaware of the faint hunger that had shown on her face. He reached out to smooth a golden curl from her cheek, his fingers cool as they brushed against her warm skin.

'You must have been very tired, Beth. You were fast asleep when Maggie came to tell you it was time for dinner. You never even stirred when I came to bed.'

There was a silky-smooth note to his voice which made her blood flow faster. She glanced at the rumpled pillow next to hers, imagining what it had been like to have his head resting there beside hers. Memory surfaced, suddenly, vividly, and she gasped. She'd thought it was just a dream, but had it been real? Had she slept in David's arms last night, warm and secure, her body curled tightly against his?

'Starting to remember now, are you, Beth?' The answer was there in his voice, glimmering in his eyes, and she flushed. He laughed deeply, tracing a long finger down her cheek and across her mouth. 'For someone who was so reluctant to share a bed you seemed to adapt to the idea very quickly.'

'David, I . . .' She couldn't think what to say. She could only stare at him, her eyes huge.

'You . . . what? Want to tell me what a heel I am for taking advantage of you?' He shook his head so that a drop of water from his wet hair fell on to her shoulder. Beth jumped and looked down, suddenly conscious of the fact that the covers had slipped to her waist, leaving the upper part of her body bare apart from the lacy black slip which she'd worn under her dress yesterday.

David's eyes followed hers, his hand sliding down to the bare curve of her shoulder as it wiped the drop away, then stayed to stroke back and forth across the soft white skin. 'You were quite safe with me last night, Beth. All I did was hold you in my arms, nothing else.'

'I . . .' His touch was making her dizzy, that slow, deliberate caress sending flames licking along her veins. 'I know that. What else would I imagine? You made your feelings very plain last night.'

His hand stilled, resting warmly on the point of her shoulder. 'What do you mean?'

She laughed shortly, more bitterness than amusement in the sound. 'I mean that you made it perfectly plain that I would be unlikely to drive you wild with lust!'

'Did I? I can't imagine how you got that idea. I think your mind must have been playing tricks.' His hand moved again, skimming over her skin to slide under the thin strap of her slip and draw it down.

Beth gasped, reaching wildly to stop him, but he gently yet firmly moved her hand aside and drew the lace away from the ripe fullness of her breast. Beth closed her eyes, hating him for teasing her this way, then felt desire spiral through her when she felt his tongue stroke moistly across her nipple.

'No! David, don't. You mustn't. It's wrong!' Her hands went to his head, her fingers burrowing into the damp silkiness of his hair to push him away, but then his mouth opened over her breast to draw the nipple further between his lips and she stilled.

Time after time he stroked the rigid nipple with his tongue and Beth moaned softly, arching towards him. When he moved away she whimpered and tried to hold his face to her, but he murmured soothingly, his hands sure and gentle as he slid the lace from her other breast. Beth felt the first light sweep of his tongue against her flesh and twisted helplessly, her hands clenching as he drew the taut bud between his teeth and grazed it gently.

Her hands slid from his head down the strong column of his neck to his shoulders, feeling the hardness of the muscles under the warm satin skin. He raised his head from her breast and captured her mouth then in a swift, possessive kiss which stole her breath and every last vestige of resistance.

Beth kissed him back, her hands clinging, stroking up and down the powerful line of his back while she felt the shudder which rippled through him with a surge of triumph. When he pushed the covers aside she made no attempt to stop him at first until she felt his fingers caressing the very heart of her femininity.

Her eyes flew open, wide, frightened, her whole body stiffening, but he stared back at her, his grey eyes calm and level. 'I want you, Beth.'

'No. You mustn't! It's wrong, David. Wrong! There's no point pretending otherwise.' Her eyes closed on a wave of sadness then shot open again when she felt his lips cover hers again in a kiss of such tenderness that it made her ache, made the throbbing need intensify.

'Pretending, Beth? Do I look as if I'm pretending?' He caught her hand, holding her eyes as he slid it down his chest and pressed it against the aroused hardness of his body through the folds of the damp towel. 'Does it feel as if I'm pretending?'

Her face coloured hectically and he laughed deeply, his eyes gleaming with amusement. 'I see you get the picture. So do you still think that it's wrong when you know how much I want you?'

'David, I...'

'What? Tell me, love.' He slid down beside her on the bed, curving her into his arms to press her so close that she could feel the hardness of him against her soft flesh.

'This is wrong,' she whispered brokenly, repeating the words in a helpless attempt to convince herself as much as him.

He smiled, his lips brushing her cheek, making the skin tingle with awareness. 'We're married. How can it be wrong?' His hand glided down her back, his fingers caressing the ridges of her spine before curling intimately around the curve of her bottom, and she shuddered helplessly.

'David, please!'

'Please...what? Hold you closer, kiss you again, show you how much I really want you? It will be my pleasure, sweet.' He drew her even closer, so close that her bare breasts were crushed against the hard, warm wall of his broad chest. Beth could feel the double beat of their hearts tapping out their rhythm and suddenly she was lost. What did it matter why he held her like this, why he kissed her, why he should claim to want her? Nothing had ever felt as right or as wonderful as being held in David's arms like this and having him love her.

She relaxed against him, her body going pliant in his hold, her arms holding him just as tightly as he held her. Why keep on denying something that was true: she wanted him just as much as he seemed to want her, wanted him with a desire that went beyond the bounds of right or wrong or reason.

'Beth.' Her name was soft on his lips, almost as soft as the kiss he gave her, and she felt her heart go still. He kissed her now not with that wild, hot passion which had set her on fire, but with an aching tenderness which made her tremble. How could one sweet kiss wipe away all the doubts and pain? She couldn't understand it, but it was so. David kissed her now and suddenly she knew without a shadow of a doubt that this was right.

The soft sound of someone knocking on the door was a cruel intrusion. Beth drew in a shuddering breath, her arms tightening around him for one desperate moment before they fell to her sides. He stared down at her, his eyes still clouded with desire, then slowly bent to rest his forehead against hers for a moment in a gesture of defeat. 'I don't believe it! Talk about bad timing.'

Beth smiled faintly, resisting the urge to draw him closer and ignore the intrusion. 'Are you going to answer or shall I?'

He shook his head, mockery on his face now as he straightened, but there was no denying the warmth lingering in his eyes as he ran a glance over her as she lay against the pillows, her hair a tangle of red-gold silk, her bare breasts rosy-tipped. 'No, you stay there. I don't want to spoil the delightful picture you make.'

Beth blushed, pulling the covers up to shield herself, warmed by the gentle teasing.

'I hope I didn't wake you up. I've brought you some tea. How is Beth this morning?'

David took the tray Maggie was carrying, pushing the door back with one bare foot as he glanced back over his shoulder at Beth. 'She's fine. All she needed was a good night's sleep...and a little tender, loving care!'

Maggie smiled. 'Stop that, David! You're embarrassing her. Right, breakfast is any time you want it. Don't rush. I was planning a nice lazy day. It will be hectic enough tonight.' She looked at Beth, her eyes warm with understanding as she met Beth's embarrassed ones. 'I hope you don't mind, but we decided to throw a party tonight. It will be mainly friends and very informal.'

'It sounds lovely, Maggie. Thank you. If you need any help then just tell me. I'll be only too glad to help you get things ready.'

'I might just take you up on that. See you later.' With a wave, Maggie hurried away, and David closed the door then carried the tray to the bedside table and set it down. He studied Beth's flushed face for a moment then moved away to open the wardrobe and take out trousers and a sweater. Dropping them on to the bed, he took clean underwear from the chest of drawers then unfastened the towel from around his waist and let it drop to the floor.

Beth felt her breath catch as she stared at him, magnificent in his nakedness. She closed her eyes, heat rippling in a tidal wave along her veins, but it was impossible to blank the image of him from her mind.

'All right, you can look now. You won't see anything you obviously feel you shouldn't.' There was open amusement in his tone and Beth opened her eyes and glared hotly at him. 'I can't help it if I'm not used to having naked men parading in front of me!'

'Indeed you can't. Frankly, I'm rather glad that you're not. Your innocence is delightfully refreshing, Beth.'

'Innocence?' She went ashen. 'Is that some sort of a joke? I lost my claim to innocence a while back as well you know!'

His face hardened. 'That's not true. Innocence is as much a state of mind as a physical condition.'

'Then you must be the only person who thinks so!' She pulled the slip back over her breasts then tossed back the bedcovers and climbed out to face him across the room with eyes filled with pain. 'You tell anyone what happened to me, David, and then ask their opinion as to whether I can be called an innocent ... Matthew ... Maggie ... anyone. They'll soon tell you how wrong you are!'

'It has nothing to do with anyone else. Not Matthew nor Maggie... no one!'

'Why? Why don't you want anyone to know? Why are you so determined to keep it all such a secret? You were talking about making this marriage of ours real yesterday, but what does that mean? That you keep on hiding the truth? Keep up this pretence that you were the father of my baby?

Why? To spare my feelings, or for your own reasons?'

'What I decide to tell people is my business, Beth. Understand? Don't interfere in things you know nothing about!'

There was such anger on his face that she almost faltered, but pain and a deep, bitter disappointment drove her on. 'Oh, I understand all right. Only too well. As long as our relationship keeps within the limits you set for it then that's fine, but let me go beyond that and... Well, I'm sorry, David, but that isn't how I want to live the rest of my life. I don't want to accept hospitality from your family in exchange for a pack of lies.'

'So what do you suggest? That you tell Matthew the truth, all of it, every unsavoury little detail?' He came and caught her by the arms, his fingers biting into her flesh. 'I don't think so, Beth. I don't think so at all. Why rock the boat? We could have a pleasant future together. I can provide for your every need and we've already proved this morning that we find one another attractive enough to guarantee an excellent physical relationship. Why ruin that by going against my wishes? Be sensible, Beth, and ask yourself what more you want from a relationship than what I'm offering.'

What more could she want? Beth went cold with despair. There was so much she wanted from David now, more than she had ever wanted from anyone before: truth, honesty, the right to share his life, plus the one thing she knew he could never give her... love.

She pulled her arms away, walking swiftly towards the bathroom. 'I'd better get dressed. Maggie will wonder what's happened to us.'

'I don't want you to tell either Maggie or Matthew anything about the terms of our marriage. Understand?'

She looked round, her face bleak, all the brightness faded. 'Oh, I understand, David. Don't worry. I shall stick to our agreement this weekend. You've set the guidelines and I shall follow them to the letter.'

She walked into the bathroom and closed the door, leaning against it as a wave of sick despair washed over her. In the space of one short hour she'd gone from the dizzy heights of happiness back into black despair, but this time she knew that it would be even harder to struggle out now that she'd had that magical taste of what life could be like.

There was no sign of David when she left the bathroom. Slipping on black trousers and a white cotton shirt, Beth went downstairs, aware of the silence in the house. She paused at the bottom of the staircase then made her way along the dark hall to the kitchen, smiling with a determined brightness when she found Maggie in there sitting at the table, a cup of coffee in one hand and a plump red-haired baby cradled on her lap. She looked up when she heard the door opening, smiling warmly when she saw Beth.

'I hope you didn't think you *had* to get up, Beth. You could have stayed in bed as long as you wanted to.'

Beth sat down at the table, reaching out to touch the baby's hand with a wistful smile. 'I didn't want to lie there any longer. I had more sleep last night than I've had in weeks. You must think me awfully rude for missing dinner last night.'

'Not at all. You obviously needed the rest.' Maggie skimmed an assessing look over her face, her green eyes darkening in faint concern. 'You still look a bit pale. Are you sure you aren't trying to overdo things, Beth?'

Beth shrugged, wishing she could confide in Maggie and tell her the truth of what ailed her, but, remembering David's warnings, she knew she couldn't do that. Once she'd recovered her strength she would have to start thinking about her future, working out if she could carry on with this strange marriage under the terms David had laid down. If she couldn't then she would have to make a decision to end it there and then, but it wasn't going to be a simple decision to make. David had come to mean so much to her; leaving him would be agonisingly painful.

'Beth?'

She jumped when Maggie spoke, realising that the other woman was still waiting for an answer. 'Sorry. I was miles away. I expect I am being a bit impatient, but I hate sitting around as though I'm an invalid. I feel fine most of the time.' She glanced at the baby, pain flashing briefly in her eyes. 'It hurts, of course. It's bound to. But physically I shall be right as rain in a week or so. It's just a question of learning to pace myself.'

'And that's the hardest thing to learn!' Maggie stood up and placed the baby on Beth's knee with a gentle smile before turning to pick up the coffee-pot and pour her a cup. She carried it back to the table, setting it down in front of her, her face filled with understanding. 'I know it must be hard for you, Beth, trying to come to terms with your loss. I keep trying to imagine what it must be like.' She shuddered, running a loving hand over the baby's downy head. 'Thank God you've got David to lean on. We're both lucky in that respect, having such strong men behind us. If it had happened to me the first time, when I had Janey when Matthew wasn't around, I don't know how I would have coped.'

Beth smiled sadly, snuggling the warm little body close, aching inside for what she'd lost. 'You would have, Maggie. The strength to go on comes from deep inside. It's there waiting to be tapped even though we're not aware of it most of the time. But when you said Matthew wasn't around, what did you mean? Was he away somewhere?'

She asked the question unthinkingly, her thoughts turned inwards, trying to imagine what it would have been like to be holding her child like this in her arms. It was almost more than she could bear, to imagine that and then be forced to face the fact that it would never be. So lost in her own bitter thoughts was she that it startled her when she looked up and saw the pain on Maggie's face. 'What is it, Maggie? Have I said something to upset you?'

'No. Of course not. I . . . I was just remembering, that's all.' Maggie sat down at the table, reaching out to take Elizabeth abruptly from Beth's arms and hold her close as though she too needed comfort. 'I tend to forget that you know so little about our family history, Beth.' Her smile took any sting out of the words. 'You see, Matthew and I were divorced a few years ago. He knew nothing about the child I was expecting. In fact, he knew nothing about Janey's existence until she was almost three years old, and that is something I shall always regret and blame myself for. I should never have kept it a secret from him. He was her father and he had a right to know, no matter what our differences were!'

What could she say? Maggie obviously felt deeply about what had gone on in the past and it struck a chord in Beth's own conscience too. Should she have told Andrew about the baby? The thought lingered for the briefest moment before common sense reasserted itself. Andrew wouldn't have wanted to know; his actions had made that very plain. He was no longer a part of her life and, if she was honest, she no longer missed him.

She touched Maggie's hand, offering comfort as best she could. 'You did what you felt was best at the time, Maggie. Don't keep blaming yourself.'

'I did.' Maggie's eyes shimmered with unshed tears, but she smiled bravely, running a finger down the baby's cheek. 'I couldn't have done anything else, but I still feel guilty at times . . . as though I stole something precious from Matthew.'

'I can understand that, but how does he feel about it?'

Maggie's face softened. 'He's been marvellous. Oh, he was furious when he first found out, but he came to terms with it better than I could have hoped he would. We got married again and when I found out I was pregnant a second time he was over the moon. He never stopped fussing me the whole time I was carrying Elizabeth, in fact.'

'He must have been delighted.'

'Oh, he was, and of course it made it all far easier for me, having him there to lean on when I felt low. Of course when I was having Janey, David was marvellous. He saw me through all the bad times when I felt like giving up. He's a good man, Beth, a strong man whom you can lean on in a time of crisis.' She gave a soft little laugh. 'But I don't need to tell you of all people that.'

'No.' Beth glanced down at the cup of coffee, staring blankly at its shiny surface. David was a good man, a kind man, a man she could turn to. She'd found that out almost as soon as they'd met. Relying on him had been so easy and natural that it made her wonder what she would do in the future if she didn't have his strength to lean on.

'Well, enough of all this doom and gloom, Beth. What do you fancy to eat? You must be starving after missing dinner last night.'

Beth followed her lead, dragging her mind away from such disturbing thoughts. 'I am rather hungry.'

'Then how about scrambled eggs and toast? I'll join you in fact, although I'll forgo the toast.' She ran a hand over one hip, a wry tilt to her mouth. 'I still have a few pounds to lose.'

'There is nothing wrong with you. You look fine to me the way you are, so never mind starving yourself.' The deep voice made them both jump, Maggie smiling as she saw her husband standing in the doorway.

'You, my love, are biased. You would think I was perfect if I was still a stone overweight.'

'Probably. And I make no apologies for it.' Matthew went and kissed her cheek, his eyes filled with tenderness, before he turned to Beth and smiled politely. 'Good morning. How are you feeling today?'

Beth shifted uneasily, once more ill at ease under the dark scrutiny. She had the feeling that Matthew saw a lot that other people failed to see and it put her on edge. 'Fine, thank you. I'm sorry about last night. I hope I didn't spoil your dinner arrangements.'

His expression softened, became less distant. 'Don't give it a second thought. You need to take things easy at the moment until you're back on your feet, but if you're anything like Maggie then I expect that's the last thing you've been doing!'

Maggie grinned. 'What did I say? Isn't he the original fuss-pot? I expect David is just the same.'

Matthew's face darkened at the mention of his brother's name. Abruptly he turned away to pour himself a cup of coffee. 'Where's Janey? Is she playing outside?'

Maggie seemed to hesitate, then spoke with a strange touch of defiance in her voice. 'David has taken her to the park.'

Matthew stiffened, his hand holding the cup tightening so that Beth expected to see the china shatter with the force of it. Just for a moment bitter jealousy flashed across his face before he took a swallow of the coffee.

Beth stared at him in confusion, feeling chilled at what she'd witnessed. Why should it upset

Matthew so much that David had taken his daughter out? It made no sense, especially in view of what Maggie had told her about how she'd relied on David while she'd been carrying the child.

Obviously deeply disturbed by the tense atmosphere that filled the kitchen, Maggie got up and carried the baby over to strap her into a bouncing chair set by the table. 'I'd better make a start on breakfast. What would you like, darling? Beth and I are——' She broke off as a small whirlwind erupted into the kitchen through the back door.

'Mummy, Uncle David took me to the swings and the slide *and* came on the roundabout with me! It was great!'

'It sounds like it.' Maggie smiled at her excited daughter. 'Now how about saying hello to Beth? She's been waiting to meet you.'

The little girl turned to look at Beth, smiling shyly. Her hair was dark and curly, dancing around her glowing little face in a tangle of silky curls. Beth returned the smile then glanced at Matthew. 'She is the absolute image of you, isn't she?'

'Do you think so?' The grim expression faded slightly as he held his arms out and Janey launched herself into them, clinging hold like a monkey as he lifted her high into the air.

'I do indeed. Hello, Janey. It's nice to meet you.'

Janey smiled back, her dark eyes, so like Matthew's, studying Beth with the same kind of intensity. 'Are you my aunty? Uncle David said that you are.'

'I...yes. Yes, I am.' Beth was surprised at the warm feeling it gave her to hear that David had said that.

'Mummy said that you were going to have a baby, but that it had gone to heaven now. Are you going to have another one?'

Would she? A child that was hers...and David's. He'd told her that it would be her choice if they decided to make their marriage real and now she knew that was something she wanted more than anything. A child of David's...their child. Not to replace the one she'd lost, but a living, breathing, precious link between them.

She barely heard Maggie's hurried admonishment to her daughter as she glanced across at David, wanting only to see some reflection of how she felt, but his face was totally blank, his eyes shuttered. Beth took a slow, painful breath, letting the precious little dream fade in the face of reality. 'I expect we shall just have to wait and see what happens, Janey.'

Janey nodded wisely. 'Perhaps it will be a surprise for you, like I was for Daddy. He said that I was the best surprise he ever had.'

'That's quite enough, Janey.' Maggie's voice was sharp, but David interrupted her, speaking for the first time since he'd come into the house.

'It's all right, Maggie. She's probably doing us all a favour by speaking about it.' He smiled at the little girl. 'I'm sure that if Beth and I have another baby it will be just as good a surprise for us too, poppet.'

Beth's heart lurched at the warmth in his voice. Had she misread him before? David was adept at hiding his feelings behind that calm mask, but who was to say if he had made that offer because he too really wanted a child to cement their marriage? Joy shone on Beth's face as she looked at him across the room, but he wasn't looking at her. He was looking at his brother, his eyes cold and calculating, and in a flash she realised what a stupid, blind fool she'd been. All he'd been doing was keeping up this pretence that their marriage was a real one because he hadn't wanted Matthew to realise what a pack of lies it all was!

Fury rose inside her, hot and swift, and she stood up quickly, ignoring the startled look Maggie gave her. 'If you don't mind, Maggie, I'll skip breakfast. I've gone off the idea. I think I'll go out and get some fresh air.'

'Well…yes…of course.' Maggie glanced round the kitchen, her gaze centring on David. 'Why don't you and David walk down to the village? He can show you around.'

'No!' The refusal was far sharper than she'd intended and she felt David's eyes on her, but she refused to look at him. 'I'm sure David has things he wants to do. I'll be fine by myself.'

She turned defiantly to him, a shiver running down her spine when she saw the icy displeasure in his eyes, but there was little sign of his true feelings in his voice. 'I do have a few phone calls to make.' He glanced at Matthew, his face set. 'I take it that you don't have any objections to my using the phone in the study?'

Matthew stared back at him. 'This is as much your house as mine, so help yourself. One of the things we need to discuss this weekend is what we're going to do with the house now that Mother has decided to stay on the coast.'

David shrugged. 'Frankly, I don't give a damn what happens to it. It holds no place in my affections.'

Matthew smiled grimly. 'Then at least we agree on one thing. I'll make arrangements to have it sold when we move out if you're agreeable.'

'The sooner the better as far as I'm concerned. It will be one less link with the past.' He met and held Matthew's gaze, his face unrelenting, and Beth felt her heart ache. It was all going wrong, one thing after another, even her and Maggie's well-meaning attempts to patch things up. It wasn't going to be simple to end this bitter feud and wipe out the past, but when was it ever simple to do that? The past always had a huge influence on future events, as she herself was finding out. If she hadn't needed it so desperately David would never have helped her in the first place and she now wouldn't find herself in this intolerable position. She wanted to make their marriage real for any number of reasons, ones she wasn't brave enough to admit to as yet, but she was afraid to take that step when everything hinged on the past. If she and David had met under different circumstances how would their relationship have progressed?

There was no answer to that question so she made her way slowly from the room and along the hall, stopping abruptly when a hand closed around her arm.

'And what did you think you were playing at just now? I warned you earlier to watch what you said, Beth, and I meant it. I won't countenance you making me look like a fool in front of Matthew!'

David's fingers were bruising on her flesh, but Beth scarcely felt them as anger rose in her again. 'If anyone is making you look a fool then it's you! What are you trying to prove, David…that we have the perfect loving marriage?' She dragged her arm away, glaring defiantly at him. 'Well, carry on with your little game if that's what you want to do, but don't expect me to applaud your efforts. You make me sick with your lies.'

'I don't give a damn what you feel. What I do or don't do is none of your concern. I gave you a home, Beth, and a job when you needed them most, but what I didn't give you was a licence to pass judgement on how I conduct my life!'

'So in return for a roof over my head I have to do as I'm told, is that it?' She shook her head, the silky hair swirling like golden fire against the white shirt. 'I won't do that. I won't perpetuate this lie in front of people like Maggie who have invited me into their home!'

'I don't see that you have that much choice. It would be a simple enough matter to end our arrangement, Beth. I wonder how you would manage then…with no job and no place to live? How do you think you would cope out in that hostile world all alone?'

There was anger on his face, but it wasn't greater than she felt. How dared he say that? How dared he threaten her?

'I'd manage, David. I would manage just fine. I don't need your charity any longer. I should have left before, the last time you laid your cards on the table and told me exactly what you feel about me!' She laughed bitterly. 'I have to hand it to you: I was almost tempted to fall in with your suggestion about turning this farce into the real thing, but thank God I didn't. I've made some mistakes recently, but that would have been the biggest one I could have made! Now all I have to do is pack my things when we get back to town tomorrow night and call it quits.'

She turned and ran up the stairs, leaving him standing there. When she reached the top, something made her look back, and she felt her stomach sink when she caught a movement at the far end of the hall. Her eyes met Maggie's horrified gaze for a moment before she turned away, hardening her heart. She didn't give a damn what anyone thought. From here on in she was going to look after herself. Once she'd left David's flat tomorrow then that would be end of it all, one more bitter lesson to add to the others she had learnt recently.

CHAPTER NINE

IT WAS further to the village than Beth had expected so that by the time she rounded the last bend she was trembling from exertion. She paused for a moment to catch her breath, then forced herself to go on, feigning an interest in the few shops which lined the narrow street.

She stopped at the baker's and bought a fresh roll still warm from the oven then sat down on a bench overlooking the village green and ate it, but it was too cold to linger there for long. The wind had risen since she'd left the house, sending needle-sharp blasts of cold air into her face, and with a weary sigh she started back up the road again. When it suddenly started to rain she could have wept.

Head bowed against the icy drops, she struggled on, forcing herself to concentrate on getting back rather than on the lump of misery lodged deep in her chest. Now all her anger had faded all she felt was a numbing kind of pain that it should have to end like this. When a car skidded to a halt alongside her, she barely spared it a glance, then felt her heart stop when she recognised the man who jumped out and came round to confront her.

'What the hell are you playing at, woman? Look at you! You're soaked through. Come on.' David caught her arm to propel her towards the car, but she resisted with a strength that surprised them both.

'No! Go away. I can manage by myself. I don't need your help, David Kane...not now...not ever!'

She pushed past him, her breath coming in laboured spurts as she hurried along the road. She hated him! Hated him for being so domineering, hated him for imagining that she would accept his help again after what he'd said before, hated him for giving her hope only to snatch it away again.

'And what do you hope to achieve by this display of independence? All you'll do is tire yourself out and get a good soaking into the bargain.'

She hadn't realised he had followed her and now she rounded on him, brushing the rain from her face. 'Go away! I don't need your company, thank you.'

He pushed his hands into his pockets, hunching his shoulders against the driving force of the rain. 'I'm sure you don't, but you're getting it anyway.' He looked grimly at the leaden sky, narrowing his eyes against the downpour. 'Looks as if we're both going to get soaked.'

'You don't need to! You can get in your car and drive back to the house. I can manage by myself.'

He shook his head, scattering raindrops as he did so. 'No way. If you're going to walk then so am I.'

His face was set with determination as he walked along beside her and Beth felt herself waver. She was wet through and freezing cold so how must David feel without a coat on? She skimmed a look over the sweat-shirt he was wearing, seeing the way the soft fabric was starting to cling to his chest, outlining the hard, lean muscles. Just for a moment time rolled back to the morning, when she had stroked those muscles, smoothed her hands over his skin, and she swallowed hard.

He must have caught her look because he raised a quizzical eyebrow, shivering slightly as the wind sent an icy blast straight at them, and Beth sighed.

'This is ridiculous. You're going to catch pneumonia without a coat on.'

He slowed and unconsciously Beth did so too. 'So I catch pneumonia. Why should that matter to you, Beth?' His voice was deep and seductive—deliberately so, she knew—but she couldn't prevent the tremor which ran through her like fire through tinder. She licked her parched lips, feeling the tremor deepen when she saw the way his eyes followed the movement of her tongue.

He moved closer, his eyes strangely intent as he repeated the question. 'Why should it matter to you what happens to me, Beth? You told me before that you wanted nothing more to do with me. Have you changed your mind?'

The wind carried the scent of his damp skin into her nostrils, a scent that she had come to know over the past few weeks. That was the trouble: she knew David so intimately in some respects yet knew him not at all in anything that mattered. How could they have hoped to maintain any sort of relationship when half of the picture was blank?

She shook her head, staring up at him with sad eyes. 'I haven't changed my mind. Once we get back tomorrow I'm leaving.'

'And where will you go?' He moved in front of her, sheltering her against the wind with his own body. 'You have no place to live, so what do you intend to do?' He laughed suddenly. 'Funny, isn't it? You're worried about me catching cold and I'm worried about how you'll manage. That hardly sounds like two people who don't give a damn about each other!'

'You would feel the same about anyone, David! It's not *me* you're really concerned about.'

'No? How do you work that out?' He moved closer again, reaching out to steady her as a gust of wind made her stagger. Beth felt his hands close around her shoulders, felt the firm, hard warmth of his fingers even through the thick layer of her coat, and her heart seemed to stop.

She loved him. The realisation settled into her mind, carried on the wind, dropping with the rain, so quiet and so natural, yet filling her with its very magnitude. She loved David so much, loved him with a depth and intensity which made her finally admit that it was no new emotion. Slowly, as the days had slid into weeks, love had grown, yet she could never admit it to him. The one thing he didn't want from her was that.

She drew away, her face set as she held back the grief tearing at her heart. 'You are a compassionate man, David. You would have helped anyone in similar circumstances.'

He shook his head, his mouth curling into a faint smile. 'I can't imagine ever offering marriage to any other woman, Beth, even if her circumstances had been the same as yours. It was you I asked to marry. . . only you that I would have asked.'

She wanted to believe him so much, but there were so many things to consider that she was afraid to take what he said at face value even though her heart begged her to do so. 'Why? Why did you really marry me, David? Oh, I can accept that you wanted to help me, but marriage...' The wind whipped her hair into her face and impatiently she brushed it back. 'I fitted in with your plans somehow, but I've still no idea where or how! If you won't tell me the truth, David, then there is no way we can carry on like this.'

His face closed up, growing cold and distant in that way she'd come to hate. 'Why not accept the fact that I did what I did with the very best of intentions? My reasons don't affect you or our relationship, Beth.'

'Don't affect me? Oh, come on! I want the truth, David, once and for all. I know it has some bearing on this weekend and this feud with your brother and I want to know what it is. I am sick and tired of being left in the dark like this!'

'You know all that I am prepared to tell you. That will have to suffice.'

'Will it? Will it, indeed? I'm afraid it doesn't.' She gave a bitter little laugh and turned to walk back towards the car. 'We may as well go back to the house. We're getting nowhere standing here in the rain. Nothing has changed, David. I still intend to leave tomorrow. I've had all I can take of these half-truths.'

He caught her up, walking silently along beside her. He unlocked the car door and waited for her to get in, then slid behind the wheel, but made no attempt to start the engine. Beth wiped a hand over her wet face, her heart aching as she saw the bleakness of his expression. What right did she have to push him into telling her things he was obviously loath to tell? She wanted to be a part of his life, but there was no way she could make him accept her as such if he didn't chose to.

It took only minutes to get back to the house. David stopped the car in the drive, his hands tightening on the steering-wheel before he turned to her. 'You asked for an explanation and maybe you are right, Beth. Maybe it is time that I told you what went on.'

She'd waited for so long to hear what had happened, yet now she felt a sudden irrational fear that the truth might be the last thing she would want to know. She shivered convulsively, wishing desperately that she had never pressured him. 'It must be your decision, David.'

'I don't think it is that any longer. I think it's more a question of what's right now. You have to know, Beth, because it could affect any decisions you make as to your future.'

The fear grew and she shivered again, feeling cold to the very depths. He noticed at once, his eyes darkening in concern as he laid the back of his hand against her cheek. 'You're absolutely frozen. Let's get inside. We can talk once you're warm and dry.'

He helped her from the car and unlocked the front door, standing aside while Beth walked into the dark hall. Shrugging off her wet coat, she went to hang it on the hallstand then gasped in alarm as her foot skidded on a pool of water that had dripped on to the tiled floor.

'Beth!' His hands were firm and sure as he caught her and held her close. Beth gave a shaky little laugh, turning her startled face up to his, then felt all the laughter die as she saw the gleam in his eyes just a moment before his mouth captured hers in a searing kiss.

Joy flooded through her, filling her with strength. No matter what David told her it wouldn't change the way she felt about him. She loved him with her heart, her soul, with every fibre of her being, and once he had finished his tale then she would tell him that. From here on in there would be no lies between them, no veils pulled over the truth.

When he moved his mouth from hers she let her head rest against his shoulder in a loving, trusting gesture, then started nervously as she caught sight of Maggie standing in the door to the sitting-room.

'Sorry. I didn't mean to intrude, but I must say that I am glad to see that you've made up. I was worried about you both.' She smiled, a faintly nervous smile for a woman who was usually so confident, making Beth realise that what she'd said had been the truth. Maggie *had* been worried, strangely so, but why? Why should it bother her so much that Beth and David had quarrelled so bitterly.

Beth glanced up at David, seeking an answer, then went cold when she saw the calculated expression on his face. She drew away from him abruptly, ice settling into her heart. She'd not noticed Maggie when she'd come in, but had he? Had he seen the other woman standing there and decided to deliberately allay her obvious fears with that kiss? He'd spoken of telling her the truth, but which was more important to him—the truth or this pretence about their marriage?

She didn't want to believe it, but, once planted, the seeds of suspicion grew. She turned away abruptly and started up the stairs, wanting only to get away from this web of deceit.

'Oh, before I forget, David, there was a phone call for you. The number is on the pad and the man who phoned said that it was urgent that you contact him.'

David nodded, turning towards the study. 'Thanks, Maggie. I'll phone him back right away. Is there any chance of you making Beth some tea? She's soaked.'

'Of course. Right away.' Maggie hurried off, obviously relieved to have something to do. David waited until the kitchen door closed behind her then looked at Beth, who had stopped halfway up the stairs. 'I'll be up as soon as I'm through with making this call. We'll talk then, Beth. All right?'

Beth nodded, avoiding his eyes as she hurried up the stairs. She should have told him not to bother, not to waste his time thinking up more lies, but it seemed too much effort. She went into the bedroom and stripped off her wet clothes, then dressed quickly in dry trousers and a fluffy pale blue sweater before sitting down in front of the mirror to dry her hair. For a moment she paused to study her reflection, staring intently at the familiar features. She wasn't beautiful, but she was pretty enough. How did David see her?

She closed her eyes, trying to imagine what he saw, but it was impossible. All she could picture in her mind's eye was the expression on his face as he'd watched Maggie across the hall. Was he merely playing her for a fool? Promising to tell her the truth, but planning on yet more lies? It seemed more than likely, but he wasn't going to get away with it. She'd played the role of fool before with bitter consequences and there was no way she was going to play it again, no matter how much she might love him!

There was fire in her eyes when he came into the room, but he never noticed as he pulled fresh trousers and a sweater out of the wardrobe. Beth watched him in silence then put the hairbrush down. 'Is there something wrong?'

He dragged the sweater over his head then finger-combed his damp hair into place. 'Unfortunately, yes. That damned delivery I spent the best part of yesterday waiting for has just arrived. I'll have to go and let them unload it.'

'Now? But can't it wait until next week?'

'No. It's vital that I have the wood for Monday so that we can start on a special order. I've been waiting months for this consignment, but there's been one hitch after another. If I turn it away now then heaven knows when they'll make a second delivery.' He emptied the change from his pockets and picked up his keys. 'I'm sorry about this, Beth. I'll be back as soon as I can.'

He was gone before she could remind him that he had promised that they would talk. She picked up the brush again and drew it through her hair, feeling a cowardly sense of relief that it had been put off until later when he got back. Frankly, she wasn't that anxious now to hear what he had to say.

David still wasn't back by the time the first guests started to arrive for the party. Beth had spent the afternoon helping Maggie get things ready before finally acceding to the older woman's pleas that she should rest. She had gone upstairs and lain down on the bed, but she hadn't slept. Her mind was too active to allow her that luxury. Until David got back and they had that talk it felt as though her life was hanging in the balance. Not a thought to let her rest easily.

There were a few people in the hall when she arrived downstairs. She smiled politely at them then made her way to the kitchen, preferring to keep herself busy. Opening the kitchen door, she stopped abruptly when she found Maggie wrapped in Matthew's arms. 'Oh, excuse me.' She started to back out of the room again, colour blooming in her cheeks when she saw Matthew's amusement.

'Don't go, Beth. It's my fault for stealing some of the hostess's time. I'm sure her husband would have something to say about that!'

He left the room and Maggie laughed as she smoothed her ruffled hair. 'I never thought I'd live to see the day when Matthew would make a joke like that. He was always so jealous before that he would never have dreamed of making a comment like that! You are definitely having a good effect on him by being here, Beth.'

'Me? But why?' There was puzzlement on her face, but Maggie didn't appear to notice as she picked up a tray of canapés and rearranged them.

'Because of David, of course!' She glanced up then and something about the bewilderment in Beth's expression must have struck her. Her face went crimson and she looked away in obvious distress. 'I'm so sorry, Beth. I shouldn't have said that.'

'Said what?' Anger flashed in Beth's eyes. 'I am getting heartily sick of everyone making these veiled references to things I know nothing about! What is going on, Maggie? Tell me.'

'I...' Maggie glanced wildly round the kitchen, relief crossing her face when the front doorbell rang. 'I have to go and answer that. Would you take this tray through to the sitting-room for me, please, Beth?'

She was gone in a whirl of silk skirts and Paris perfume before Beth could stop her, hurrying along the hall. Beth picked up the tray, the light of battle shining in her eyes. This had gone on long enough; one way or another she was going to find out the truth and it didn't matter whether it was David or Maggie or whoever who told her. She was sick and tired of being left in the dark!

There were several couples in the sitting-room when she carried the tray through and set it down on the heavy, ornate sideboard. They smiled at her in a friendly manner then carried on with their conversations, leaving her to join in if she chose. Beth looked round, feeling that she should try to be sociable, but not comfortable with the thought of butting in on a stranger's conversation. However, the decision was taken out of her hands when a tall, elegant brunette detached herself from the group and came across to her.

'You must be Beth. Maggie's told me a lot about you. I'm Marie, a friend of hers and the other godmother, although it beats me why Maggie should deem me suitable for that honour!'

Beth laughed, taking an immediate liking to the woman's warm friendliness. She was very beautiful with masses of thick dark hair which swung down her back and huge dark eyes. She was also strangely familiar. Beth stared at her for a moment then gave a slightly embarrassed laugh. 'I have the feeling that I've met you before, but I can't think where.'

Marie grimaced, taking a sip of her wine before tossing her hair back and striking a deliberately sultry pose. 'The latest edition of *Vogue*? Or maybe *Paris Match*?' She grinned impishly. 'I've done extremely well recently and been on the cover of several international magazines.'

'Of course! That's where I've seen you. It must be fabulous being a model.'

Marie shrugged. 'It's a job and a well-paid one at that, but ask Maggie and she'll tell you the same thing—that it can get terribly boring at times.'

'Maggie was a model too?'

'Still is, or will be once she's back to fighting weight, although I have my doubts about whether she will really want to tear herself away from that adorable baby when the time comes. She spent such a lot of time away from Janey out of necessity that I doubt she'll want to do it this time and who can blame her?' Just for a moment sadness crossed her face before she fixed the professionally bright smile back into place. 'It might surprise you to learn that I would swap all the top modelling jobs in the world for what Maggie has. You can't beat having the man you love and his child.'

You couldn't. Beth's heart lurched at the simple truthfulness of the statement. What more could she want from life than David and his child? Deep sadness shone in her eyes and she heard Marie murmur in concern. 'Look, I'm sorry, Beth. That was a crassly insensitive thing to say in the circumstances.' She touched Beth's arm in gentle apology. 'Maggie told me about the baby you lost. It must hurt a lot.'

Beth tried to smile, but her heart was aching. She had lost her child; was she destined to lose David too? If they couldn't work things out then that would be so. There had to be a way to sort it all out. He might not love her as she loved him, but he cared something for her. He'd shown that today by coming after her down to the village. Maybe it had been partly to keep up the pretence about this marriage of theirs, but she'd seen his face, seen the genuine concern about what would happen to her if she left. There had to be something there that they could build on. To have David and maybe some day have his child to love was worth fighting for.

Suddenly she needed him with a desperation that defied all reason, needed him to be there beside her. Ignoring Marie's startled exclamation, she turned and hurried from the room and into the study to dial the factory number, letting it ring endlessly until she was forced to face the fact that David wasn't there. She replaced the receiver, her hand shaking as emotion built up inside her. She'd held back her grief about the baby for so long, yet now it all welled up, intensified by her fears for the future. A sob rose into her throat and she bit it back, terrified of breaking down in such a public place. Blinded by tears, she ran into the hall and up the stairs to her room and threw herself down on the bed, sobbing as though her heart would break.

'Beth? What is it? Don't you feel well?' Matthew's voice was tinged with concern as he came into the room and stood by the bed, and that made Beth cry all the harder. So much concern from both these men—David and now Matthew—yet none of it could help.

'Don't, Beth. You'll make yourself ill crying like that. Do you want me to get Maggie for you?'

'No.' Her voice was thick with tears, muffled by the sobs which racked her, and Matthew put a hand gently on her shoulder.

'Is it because of the baby, Beth? Is this all too much for you?'

'The baby, David, Maggie, you... It's everything, Matthew!'

His eyes darkened with concern and he sat down on the edge of the bed, gripping her shoulder tighter. 'What do you mean? How do Maggie and I have any bearing on your being upset?'

'Ask your brother. Ask David that, but of course you two aren't really talking, are you? Why? What is this big secret, Matthew? What is this skeleton you've got hidden in your cupboard?'

The thought made her giggle, the giggle rising to hysteria within the space of seconds. Matthew caught her by the shoulders and pulled her upright to shake her hard. 'Stop it, Beth. Get a grip on yourself. David will be back soon, then we can get this sorted out once and for all.'

'Will we?' Her eyes were huge, her face ashen. 'I don't know if that's what I want any longer. I don't know how I feel apart from the fact that it hurts, Matthew. It hurts!' Her head dropped forwards on to his shoulder as a weary tiredness enveloped her all at once. If only David would come then maybe it would be all right, maybe they would be able to sort everything out. David had a way of making sense out of chaos. It seemed like an answer to a prayer when she suddenly realised that he was standing in the doorway. She jumped to her feet, wanting to run to him, but he wasn't even looking at her. His eyes were locked on his brother and, even through her pain, Beth felt fear run through her when she saw the hatred in their silvery depths.

'I wondered why you agreed to this weekend, Matthew, wondered why you should want us here, and now I know. Was this all planned? Were you just waiting for the right moment to seek your revenge?' David laughed, a harsh, ugly sound that made Beth wince. 'I have to hand it to you. Even knowing you as well as I do, I never expected this particular *coup de grâce*. You're the expert, Brother, so how do you categorise this: divine law, retribution? I seduced your wife, so you planned on seducing mine to get even?'

'No!' Beth's voice was no more than a whisper when she wanted to scream the word aloud. She pressed her hands over her ears, wanting to blot out the ugly sound of David's voice saying those dreadful words, but it was impossible. They echoed inside her head, swelling to such a pitch that they seemed to fill every part of her mind so that she could think of nothing else. 'I seduced your wife.' Was it any wonder that these two men hated one another?

She backed away from them, her whole body shaking as her world fell into ruins, shattered by that one starkly cruel statement. But neither seemed to notice as they stood locked in their own private hell.

'How far were you planning on going, Matthew? Surely you didn't intend to talk Beth into bed with you, here in your own home?' He smiled, his lips drawing back into a snarl. 'Or did you? Could it be that your desire for revenge wasn't solely focused on me, but on Maggie as well? You must have lived with the thought of this for all these years, like a festering sore that needs lancing to heal, and what better way than to have her come into this room and find you here just as you came that time and found Maggie in my bed?'

David's voice was painting pictures in her head, pictures she didn't want to see, and Beth moaned in distress. David and Maggie lovers? She couldn't bear it, couldn't bear to face up to how far he'd tricked her.

She turned and ran from the room, pushing past a couple who were coming up the stairs, her one thought to get away from this nightmare. Wrenching the front door open, she raced down the drive then stood panting at the bottom with tears rolling down her face as she tried to decide where to go next.

'Beth!' His voice was harsh, cutting into the wildness of her distress, making her panic to get away. With a sharp little cry, Beth turned and ran along the road, stumbling in her high heels.

'For God's sake, stop! Stop, I say!' He caught her roughly around the waist and swung her bodily off the ground, holding her tightly as she fought wildly to get free.

'Put me down, do you hear me, David . . . put me down!' She twisted and turned in his grasp, but he was far too strong for her to break away. With a sobbing moan she went limp in his arms, her whole body shaking with emotion.

'If I put you down will you promise not to run off again?' He shook her slightly, staring down into her face. 'Beth . . . can you hear what I'm saying to you?'

She nodded, her face paper-white in the glare from a nearby streetlight. 'I can hear you, David. I've heard everything you've said since you got back. Every single word!'

His face went rigid, his eyes like pewter. 'We need to discuss what you heard, or rather, what you thought you heard, but not here. Come along.' He caught her arm to lead her back to the house, but Beth pulled back.

'No! I'm not going back there to be humiliated again!'

He glared at her, tall and dangerous-looking in the dim light. 'Nobody is going to do anything at all to hurt you, Beth. Don't be silly.'

'Silly? Is that what you think I am . . . silly? Because I object to being made to look a fool? How you must have been enjoying yourself these past few months, David, enjoying the way you were deceiving me for your own despicable purposes. No wonder you wouldn't tell me what that quarrel with your brother had been about. That really would have let the cat out of the bag, wouldn't it? And that was something you didn't dare risk or it might have upset all your plans!'

'I have no idea what you mean. I appreciate the fact that you're upset, but once we've had time to talk then you'll soon see that this has been a huge mistake.'

'Oh, will I, indeed? Why? Because you're going to tell me yet more lies? I don't think so!'

She whirled round to walk back down the road, but he caught her again and half dragged her up the drive, stopping beside his car to open the door. 'Get in.'

'And if I refuse?'

'Then, Beth, reluctant though I am to do so, I shall be forced to make you. Now spare us both that indignity and get inside.'

Beth hesitated for a moment, wanting desperately to tell him to go to hell, but there was something about the set of his jaw that warned her he would do exactly as he had said. In silence she slid into the seat and sat numbly, while he climbed behind the wheel and started the engine with an angry roar and drove out on to the road.

'Where are you taking me, David?' she demanded, harshly. 'Haven't you done enough for one night without abducting me into the bargain?'

He swore softly, cutting her a hard look as he turned the car on to the main road. 'All I want is to talk to you so that we can work this out.'

'Talk or lie? I don't think there is anything you have to say that I want to hear! I heard enough back at the house. In fact, I heard more than enough and frankly I don't want to hear another word you have to say because it will all be lies!'

'I have never lied to you, Beth. Once we've had a chance to talk then I'm sure we can work this misunderstanding out.'

'Misunderstanding?' Anger rose, bringing with it a biting pain that made her want to lash out and hurt him as he'd hurt her. 'I've heard it called some things, but a "misunderstanding"? You used me, David, to try to end a feud that you had started by sleeping with your brother's wife, and you call that a "misunderstanding"?' She laughed harshly, her face a deathly pale mask. 'I have to admire your nerve even though I hate you for what you've done!'

'I have done nothing, Beth. Nothing!'

'No? Oh, forgive me for sounding sceptical, but do you honestly expect me to believe that? You married me, David, so that you would have the perfect cover for your plans. I gave you an outward aura of respectability, helped lull everyone into thinking it couldn't happen again, but what were you really planning on? Resuming your affair with Maggie once Matthew's suspicions had been allayed? Under cover of this nice respectable marriage of ours anything would have been possible! No wonder you didn't want me to tell anyone the truth about this marriage, or about who really was the father of my baby! How could you have done that, David? How could you have used not only me but my child?'

Tears slid from her eyes, running silently down her cheeks at that cruellest of betrayals.

'No!' He slewed the car to a halt, turning in his seat to face her, his grey eyes burning with anger. 'You know damned well that isn't true, Beth!'

'I don't know anything apart from what I heard. Want me to remind you? "I seduced your wife, so you planned on seducing mine?" That seems to sum it all up, David!'

'What you heard me saying wasn't the truth. It was what Matthew had always believed, but it never happened. I never had an affair with Maggie, although lord knows I would have sold my soul to the devil at one time to do so!' He ran his hands through his hair, his voice hollow as he continued. 'The truth is that Maggie was always in love with Matthew. I never existed for her except in the role of a friend. It took me a long time to accept that, but once I did, I wasn't foolish enough to think that I could change it, nor would I hope to change it in the future.'

'And you expect me to believe that? Obviously Matthew doesn't or he wouldn't still be carrying on this quarrel. If he was confident that there was nothing between you and Maggie then he would end it here and now.'

'Would he?' He laughed shortly. 'Your faith in human nature is touching, Beth, but misplaced. I don't doubt that my brother realises that there was never anything going on between Maggie and me; she would have made sure that he did believe it. But nothing can change the fact that at one time I thought I was in love with her. He knew that only too well, and it isn't something either of us can forget easily. It's a man's nature to be possessive about the woman he loves, and Matthew loves Maggie all right.'

'And that's the real reason why you two are still enemies?' She shook her head. 'You tell a fine tale,

David Kane, but you forget that I heard every word that was said tonight...every word that *you* said! Matthew found his wife in your bed and yet you still sit there and claim that you never slept with her? Come on...spare me any more lies, please!'

'I have never lied to you, Beth, and I am not lying now.'

'I'm afraid that I don't believe you. All along the line you refused to discuss your real reasons for marrying me, but now they are so obvious. I was a convenient cover for the affair you were hoping to resume with Maggie!'

'You really think that?' He laughed scornfully, his face filled with derision. 'You've seen how Maggie looks at Matthew. She's crazy about him, just the same as she's always been.'

'Maggie's feelings aren't at question here. It's how you feel...what you were planning to do!' Suddenly she felt unable to cope any more, overcome by the horror of what had happened. 'There is nothing left to say, David. It's over, the whole foolish arrangement. I blame myself for being stupid enough to go along with it in the first place.'

'So that's it, is it? The final chapter? You refuse to believe what I am trying to explain to you, so conveniently decide that it's the end?' He leaned closer, his eyes glittering dangerously as he stared into her face. 'Now who's telling part of the truth, Beth?'

'I don't know what you mean.' She edged over in her seat, disturbed by the intensity of his gaze.

'Don't you?' He captured her chin, tilting her face so that she was forced to suffer the icy scrutiny.

'Maybe tonight is just the moment you've been waiting for, a convenient way of getting yourself out of this obviously unwanted marriage in a fashion that means you can avoid any of the blame? What are *you* planning on doing now, Beth? Contacting Andrew again and resuming your affair with him? Without the encumbrance of the baby, I'm sure he would be more than willing to agree!'

It was so far from the truth that she could have wept. She'd barely spared Andrew a thought for days now. He was from her past and the last thing she ever wanted was to see him again. Not because she felt bitter about how he had treated her, but because he no longer meant anything to her. David was all she had wanted in her future; David was all she would ever want, but it seemed it wasn't to be. Maybe the best way to end this pain which was tearing her apart was by using the solution he had offered to her.

'Yes. That's right. I'm going to contact him again and see if we can pick up where we left off! You aren't the only one who can make plans, David!'

His fingers gripped her chin for a moment, so hard that she had to bite her lips to stop herself crying out. For a silent second, he stared at her, then let her go, starting the car and pulling away from the kerb with a harsh squeal of tyres. Beth sat back in her seat, trembling all over from that fleeting look which had seemed to cut straight to her heart. David was the one who had betrayed her trust; so why did she feel so guilty, as though she was the one who had betrayed *him*?

They drove back to town in total silence until David stopped the car in the driveway of the flats, his voice hard when he spoke. 'You do have your key?'

Beth shook her head, not trusting herself not to start crying. 'It's in my coat back at Maggie's. I...I didn't have chance to get it.'

He said nothing, merely switched off the engine and unfastened his key from the ring and held it out to her. 'You'd better use this, then, to let yourself in.'

'Aren't you coming in, then?' She searched his face, desperate even now to see something that would make her change her mind and realise that she'd made a dreadful mistake, but the mask he wore so often was firmly back in place.

'No. I shall have to go back. There are things that need sorting out and now is the time to do it.' He slid the key back into the ignition and started the engine again, turning to look at her, and Beth felt her heart contract. Sitting there with him, his face shadowed by the dim glow from the dashboard, it was hard not to imagine that tonight had all been some horrible dream. He looked the way he always did, the way she pictured him whenever she closed her eyes, but the outward image belied the true character of the man.

'You go on inside, Beth. I'll be back later. Don't wait up for me.'

She nodded and climbed out of the car, watching until the rear lights disappeared, then took a slow, steadying breath as she walked towards the door. It was over. Now all that was left was to tidy up any loose ends. When he got back she would be gone.

CHAPTER TEN

THE sky was leaden, huge black clouds oozing over the skyline, threatening another downpour. Beth drew her coat collar tightly under her chin and hurried along the street, anxious to get into work before the rain set in. It was only a short walk from the drab little room she rented to the estate agent's office where she worked, but she was already cold, her fingers numb from the icy wind. Winter had arrived with a vengeance, bleak and grey, matching the bleakness in her heart.

The office was quiet that morning, just a few telephone enquiries concerning property which had been viewed at the weekend. Beth handled what enquiries she could, then passed the rest on to her boss and carried on with typing out the details of a house that was to be put on the market. A lot of the work she did was boringly repetitive, but it was enough for her to manage, enough to pay the rent on the room. Most of the time she felt as though she was existing in some kind of limbo, going through the motions of living a life which held no interest for her any longer. All the joy and colour of truly living had died that night she'd learned how David had used her.

Her eyes clouded for a second, the words blurring on the page, and she took a slow, deep breath as she waited for the agony to pass as she knew it would. She tried to stop herself from thinking about

David, but just sometimes a thought would slide unbidden into her mind, a thought so rawly painful that it left her shaking. They said time healed, but several months had passed and the wounds were still raw and open. It would take more than time to wipe David from her mind and from her heart.

The door opened, sending a flurry of cold air across the room to where she sat behind the desk. Beth looked up from her work, fixing a smile to her mouth, then felt her stomach lurch when she recognised the couple who had come in.

'Beth! Oh, Beth, I don't believe it's you at last. We've looked everywhere for you and now here you are!' Maggie's face was alight with joy, her green eyes gleaming with evident relief as she ran across the room and caught Beth's cold hands in hers. For a moment Beth sat still, stunned by the unexpected meeting, then slowly drew away.

'Hello, Maggie. How are you?'

'Never mind about me, it's you we want to hear about! We almost tore this city apart trying to find where you'd gone to after you left the flat!'

Beth looked away from the glittering green gaze which held a concern she didn't want to see. She didn't want anything from anyone now. She wanted to live her life on her own, locked into this state of limbo. It hurt far less this way. 'There was no reason for me to stay. You must know that.'

'But why just disappear? You must have realised how concerned we would all be after what happened. David has been half out of his mind with worry, wondering what had happened to you.'

David. The name slid past the barriers she'd tried so hard to erect and she drew in a ragged little breath. 'I'm sure David isn't the least worried about what happens to me. I'm no longer his concern.'

'You're wrong! You must see him, Beth, speak to him, try to sort this out. He——'

'I think that is Beth's decision, Maggie.' Matthew's voice was stern as he came to stand beside his wife, but Maggie didn't seem at all convinced.

'Maybe it is. But I'm not wholly certain that she's capable of making the right decision!'

'And this isn't the time nor the place to discuss it.' He took her arm, steering her away from Beth's desk towards the door which separated the showroom from the offices. 'We have an appointment to keep, Maggie. Let's get that over and done with first and then see what can be done to sort this mess out.' His tone brooked no argument, his face set into uncompromising lines as he ushered Maggie ahead of him through the door. He paused to glance back at where Beth was sitting ashen-faced. 'She is right, though, Beth. You have to see David and try to talk this through. I made a mistake a few years back by being stubborn, which almost cost me Maggie. Don't let that happen to you and David. Pride is a cold and lonely companion, Beth.'

The door swung to and Beth sank back in the chair, feeling her heart thumping in a rhythm that made her feel sick. She didn't want to try to sort things out by seeing David. She wanted to be left alone and not be reminded of all she'd lost. Nothing that either Maggie or Matthew could say would change what had happened and the way that David had used her. The rift between them now was far too great to be healed by words.

She stood up abruptly, snatching her bag from the drawer. It was almost lunchtime so she would leave the office and pray that they were gone by the time she got back. She couldn't face a repeat of Maggie's well-meaning attempts to help, especially in view of the fact that Maggie was at the very heart of what had caused all the trouble.

She walked round for well over an hour, wandering aimlessly along the crowded streets until finally she was forced to go back. Her boss would take a very dim view of her leaving early and then being late back. She couldn't afford to jeopardise this job when she needed it so much to support herself. In the first couple of weeks after she'd left David she'd been forced through necessity to use some of the money he had paid her, but since she'd got this job she hadn't touched another penny. She couldn't bear the thought of taking anything that had been his.

The office was empty when she got back into work and she settled down at her desk with a feeling of relief. It had been such a shock seeing them so unexpectedly, but hopefully that would be the end of it. Her marriage to David was over and once he arranged the divorce, as he surely would soon, then that would be that. There would be no reason for them to meet again.

She was cold and wet by the time she arrived home. The rain had come down as it had been threatening to do all day, heavy deluges of water swirling across the pavements. Beth slid her key into the front door and let herself into the house, sighing as she shook the water from her coat. The house was divided into a dozen rooms and as she climbed the stairs she could hear the ever-present sound of other tenants' televisions, smell the stale, lingering odour of food that always seemed to hang in the air.

Reaching the third-floor landing, she dug into her pocket for her key, then jumped when she heard a man's voice saying her name. She spun round at once, her face ashen as she recognised David standing in the shadows.

'What do you want?' There was scant politeness in the abrupt question and his face tightened before he moved towards her across the narrow hall.

'To speak to you, of course.'

'I have nothing I want to say to you, not now, not ever!' She was holding the key so tightly that it bit into her fingers, but she welcomed the pain to help her keep a grip on her control. 'I suppose Maggie sent you. It's just a pity that she doesn't confine her interest to people who would welcome it!'

He shook his head, a strange expression flashing across his face. 'She didn't tell me that she'd seen you. It was Matthew who telephoned me.'

'Oh.' That surprised her so that for a moment she faltered before gathering herself once more. 'Then I'm afraid he had a wasted phone call. Goodbye, David.'

She jammed the key into the lock, her hand shaking so hard that she couldn't seem to turn it. David pushed her hand aside and took hold of the key to unlock the door then handed it back to her, his face set and uncompromising. 'We have to talk, Beth. There's no point in being ridiculous about this. Surely we can act like two sensible adults for a few minutes while we sort this out?'

'Talk? About what? What I heard at Maggie's house that night, the truth that you had been keeping hidden from me so successfully? Forget it, David. You and I have done all the talking we are ever going to do. Frankly, you made yourself more than plain that night!' There was no disguising the raw agony in her voice as the barriers started to fall one by one, leaving her defenceless against the pain.

'You can't still believe that I tricked you, Beth? That the whole of our marriage was set up for one reason and one alone, so that I could make a play for Maggie? Come on, where's your common sense? You know that isn't true!'

Anger ran through his voice, but Beth ignored it, caught up in the spiral of her misery. 'I know what I heard!'

'Do you indeed?' He swore softly, elbowing the door open to push her inside the room. Beth backed away from him, fear running through her when she saw the naked fury on his face. He skimmed a glance around the threadbare room, distaste showing briefly in his eyes before he looked coldly back at her. 'I find it hard to believe that you prefer this to the comfort of the flat. What have you been trying to achieve by hiding out here, Beth? Were you hoping to punish me in some way for those supposed misdeeds I've perpetrated?' He laughed harshly. 'Seems to me that the only person who's been suffering is you, living here in this...this hovel when you could have been living in luxury and comfort at the flat!'

His cruel assessment of her home stung and she glared back at him, no longer afraid. 'This "hovel", as you call it, is my home, David. If you don't like it then you can always leave. In fact, I would be delighted if you would do so right now!'

She moved towards the door, but he stopped her as she drew level with him, his hand closing around the slender bones in her wrist. 'I shall leave when I am good and ready to and not before. I didn't come here tonight to play more silly games with you. I came to sort this situation out once and for all.'

'There is nothing to sort out.' She wrenched her hand away, rubbing her skin where his fingers had left an imprint. 'You used me as a cover to restart your affair with Maggie. That's all there is to it, and nothing...not one single word...will make me believe any differently.'

'Why? Why won't you at least spare a few minutes to hear me out? Afraid that you might start to doubt what you claim to believe? Afraid that your excuse for leaving me might be damaged in some way?' He looked around himself, scorn evident in the set line of his law. 'It surprises me that Andrew lets you live here. Doesn't he find such humble surroundings somewhat daunting to his ardour? After all, he can't take you home, can he? Not when his wife is there.'

The cruelly mocking words sent caution winging out of the window. 'Andrew has nothing to do with where I live. He's never been here and I have absolutely no intention of inviting him!'

His expression altered subtly, his eyes gleaming in a way that made her immediately regret her impetuous statement. 'Haven't you indeed? Yet you led me to believe that was your intention, that you were going to contact him again and pick up where you left off? What went wrong, Beth? Wasn't he willing . . . or was that all a pack of lies?'

The way he was watching her was making her nervous, making the blood rush to her head, making her skin prickle in a silent warning. In her heart she knew she should try to calm down and keep this meeting as low-key as possible, but it was impossible now that David had loosed all these emotions inside her. For all these weeks she'd lived in that strange state of limbo and now she was coming abruptly out of the trance. 'Yes! It was all lies . . . every bit of it. I couldn't give a damn if I never saw Andrew ever again. He means nothing to me, David Kane, absolutely nothing!'

'Is that right? Then why did you tell me all those lies, Beth?' His voice was soft all of a sudden, so soft that it shocked her when what she'd expected had been anger. She started nervously, licking her dry lips as she stared back at him, trying to understand this sudden shift in attitude, and felt heat scorch her face when she saw the sensuous gleam in his eyes as they rested on her mouth. Suddenly the tension in the room took on a new form, a form that scared her more than what had been between them before. She didn't want to look at David and see that he *wanted* her; she didn't want to be reminded of how much she had once wanted him! She loved him so much and it would be so easy to let him talk and persuade her in whatever direction he wanted her to go. But she'd been used once by him and she wouldn't be used again.

'It doesn't matter what I said or why, David. Just tell me why you came here tonight.'

'Just to talk to you. To explain again what you overheard and how wrong you were in your assumptions of what went on. Would it help convince you any, Beth, if I told you that Matthew and I are now on speaking terms?' He saw her surprise and smiled almost bitterly. 'Oh, I'm not going to lie and say that we are close. We shall never be that, but, there again, we never were that close, even as children. But at least we can stay in the same room and hold a civilised conversation and the reason for this is that Matthew has finally admitted that he was wrong. If he can accept the truth, Beth, then why can't you?'

Could she? Could she wipe away all the doubts which filled her mind, accept that David had never had an affair with Maggie? It would take strength to do that, possibly more strength than she possessed. Could David give her that strength? Possibly.

'Why does it matter to you that I should accept it? What do you want with me, David? If you wanted to see for yourself that I'm all right then you've achieved that much. What else did you come here for?'

'To ask you to come back with me, Beth.'

'Why?' Her voice was a tiny whisper, choked by the sudden flare of hope that he might give her the answer she wanted to hear, the only answer that would make her agree.

'Because we could still have a good life together. To just stand aside and let that all be ruined over a silly misunderstanding seems little short of a crime to me. So, what do you say, Beth? Will you try again to make our marriage work?'

'No!' Hope had stolen her voice; disappointment and a grief so sharp that it cut into her heart turned the answer into a total refusal that he must have known immediately was final. His face darkened and he turned away, wrenching open the door and walking out without another word. Beth watched him go as tears slid down her cheeks, knowing that there would never be another chance. It was such a wicked waste, such a cruel, deliberate blow from fate to have given her that one too brief moment of hope then snatch it away.

If David had just said that he loved her she would have accepted there and then, without a thought for what had happened in the past, just joy for what would happen in the future.

'You little monkey. Look at this mess!' Maggie picked up the spilled dish of food and glared at her smiling little daughter. 'And don't think that you can get round me like that, young lady!'

Beth laughed as she lifted the smiling child from her high chair. She cuddled her close, feeling the tiny pain she always felt when she held Elizabeth and remembered her own baby. It made her wonder if she was right to keep on accepting Maggie's invitations to her house, but it was always so hard to refuse, not only because she valued Maggie's friendship, but because she was her one last link with David. It might be foolish to cling to such a link even now, but somehow she couldn't quite sever it.

'Right, give me the little monster and I'll wash her face and put her down for a sleep. Then maybe we can have half an hour to ourselves, seeing as you've managed to get a day off from work.' Maggie lifted the happily squirming child high in the air then cuddled her close, muttering loving threats as to what she'd do next time she threw her dish on to the floor. Beth watched them leave the room, then stood up to fill the kettle, trying to ignore the hollow ache at what she'd lost.

'Are you OK? You look . . . well, sad.' There was genuine concern in Maggie's voice as she came back into the room, and Beth tried to smile. 'Of course. I was just going to make some coffee. Is that all right?'

'Yes. Fine.' Maggie put her hand on her arm. 'Were you thinking about your baby just now?'

'Yes. It's just sometimes that it hurts so much, like when I see you holding Elizabeth and realise what I've lost.'

Maggie gave her a fierce hug. 'I wish there was something I could say or do to help, but there isn't, is there? I'm sure that David feels it too.' She saw Beth's expression and continued determinedly. 'Look, I haven't mentioned this before, but I know about David not being the baby's father. Oh, I probably don't know it all, just what David told Matthew the night of the party.' She closed her eyes for a moment. 'What a night that was! I was downstairs, trying to be the life and soul to keep everyone happy, worried sick about you, and David and Matthew were upstairs going at it hammer and tongs. I never want to go through anything like that again, but in a way it was worth it. It finally cleared the air, Beth, and that was something I'd been praying would happen for a very long time. I'm just so desperately sorry that it broke you and David up. Are you sure there is no way that you two will get back together again? He worries about you, you know. Every time he phones, he asks if I've seen you and how you are.'

Warmth flooded through her, but deliberately Beth hardened her heart. There was no point in deluding herself, as Maggie was so obviously doing. 'I can't imagine why he should even mention me, frankly. I fail to see why David is the least bit interested in what I do.'

'The same as you aren't interested in him?' Maggie laughed lightly. 'I suppose I could try and tell myself that it's just my friendship that brings you here, Beth, but we both know that's not so! It's just a pity that the pair of you are so pig-headed. For heaven's sake, Beth, why don't you just admit that you're in love with the man? At least that would be a step in the right direction!'

Beth stiffened. 'And which direction would that be? Along the road to more heartache. No, thanks! I've had my share of that.'

'Because of the baby's father?'

Colour flamed in Beth's face, but she held her head up proudly. 'That is well in the past. I never think about him now, if you want the truth. I had a lucky escape and my only excuse is that I was both gullible and lonely when I met him.'

'Then if it isn't him you must mean David. You are in love with him, aren't you, Beth? I can tell the signs, how you cling to every word when I speak about him although you try your hardest to hide the fact. Love can be a stinker when it goes wrong, but sometimes all it takes is a bit of courage. Why don't you tell David how you feel? You might be surprised at his reaction.'

'I doubt that very much! Oh, David did come round to see me and asked me to go back to him, but do you want to know why? Because he felt we could have a good life together. That was it, nothing more. I suppose I should be grateful he didn't try to lie about how he felt, but it isn't enough, Maggie. I want more than that!'

'Maybe he would like to offer more but is frightened to make the first move. Do you know he phoned the other night, long-distance from Dallas, and guess what was the first thing he said: had I seen you?'

'That...that means nothing. You're just looking for a happy ending, but there isn't going to be one. David doesn't love me. If he loves anyone at all then it's you!' She expected Maggie to be annoyed at the accusation. What she hadn't expected was that she would throw back her head and laugh.

'Me? No way! Maybe he did imagine something of the sort a while back, but that's not how he feels now. I think you should ask yourself a few little questions and the first one should be why it is that neither of you has started divorce proceedings. Seems strange to me!'

Maggie threw her ace flat on the proverbial table then promptly changed the subject, but it was impossible for Beth to brush the challenge aside as she would have liked to. When she left Maggie's house, she started walking, letting her feet carry her where they would, yet when she found herself outside the front door to the flats where David lived she wasn't surprised. This was where it had all started that day when he had first helped her; would this be where she would find the answers?

She let herself into his flat, feeling safe in the knowledge that he was still thousands of miles away in Dallas. It had been months since she'd been there, but, as she stood in the quiet hall, all those days faded as the familiarity of the place welcomed her back. She closed her eyes, letting the memories seep into her mind, but they weren't enough to live on in the future. She wanted David, the real man, the man who had helped her, held her, kissed her, made her fall in love with him. She wanted David back in her lonely life under any terms. She had been a fool to refuse to come back to him. She could have lived with him and maybe some day have taught him to love her in return.

She walked through the flat, recalling snatches of conversation they'd had, moments which had seemed insignificant then, but seemed so important now they were all she had. But it was when she stopped in the doorway to the room she'd used that everything crystallised into bitter-sharp focus when she saw the work-box lying on the bed.

She went over to it, trailing her fingers over the silky smoothness of the polished wood, tracing the pattern of roses wound round her initial. David had made this for her; surely it must mean something?

'Beth.' His voice was from the past and the present, linking them both. It didn't startle her, just fitted in with her thoughts. Beth turned slowly, aware that if he looked close enough he would see everything she felt for him, but it didn't matter. Now wasn't the time to hide.

'What are you doing here?' There was ice in his deep voice and some of the memories started to disintegrate and re-form into far more bitter ones. She drew herself up against the ensuing pain, facing him across the room, but it might as well have been across a huge chasm. There was such hostility in his eyes that it would be impossible to bridge such a huge gap with memories and wishes.

'I didn't think that you would be here,' she said quietly.

'I only got back this morning.' He raked his hair back from his brow, his eyes flat. 'What did you want, Beth? Why did you come here?'

Beth drew in a shuddery breath as the last of the warmth faded. What if Maggie had been wrong in her advice? How could she just stand there and tell him that she loved him and hope that it would all turn out right? That was the stuff of fairy-tales, not real life.

Fear tied her tongue so that she could only stand and stare at him, and she heard him mutter something harsh under his breath. He swung round and left the room, his footsteps echoing as he moved along the hall. Beth stood still, listening to her heart pounding in the silence. What should she do? Leave, or stay and face this out? Was she really such a coward that she wouldn't fight for what she wanted from life?

Her heart was thumping hard and fast, but she made herself walk steadily into the sitting-room. David was standing by the window, his arm raised against the frame as he stared out. He didn't look round when she entered the room, but she could tell that he had heard her by the way his body tensed.

'Well, ready to tell me what this is all about?' His voice cracked like a whip and Beth jumped. She glanced round, then went and sat down on a chair, forcing herself to remain calm.

'It was just an impulse that brought me here,' she said softly. 'I never expected you to be home, but, seeing as you are, I think we should talk.'

'Oh, do you, indeed? That makes a change. The last time we met you stated quite clearly that you couldn't see any reason for us to talk as everything had already been said! What makes you think that things have changed, Beth?'

His cold sarcasm hurt, but Beth steeled herself to ignore it. 'I remember what I said, David. I was wrong. We need to talk.'

'About what? The weather, the balance of payments? Name the topic, Beth, then we can have this "talk" before you leave!'

The pain she felt was intense as she heard the diamond hardness of his voice mocking her, but she blocked the pain from her mind. 'Us.'

He turned then, his eyes skimming over her in a swift, all-encompassing glance that seemed to strip her to her soul. 'Us? I didn't think there was an "us" any longer. I asked you to come back to me and you refused. End of subject.'

'It isn't the end! What's the matter, David? Did I wound that stiff pride of yours by refusing your magnanimous offer that day?' Her eyes flashed defiance at him although she could see the growing anger on his face.

'What you did, Beth, was give me an answer. I don't see that there is anything left to discuss.'

'Oh, don't you? Don't you think it would be fairer to both of us if you stopped being so pig-headed before it ruins both our lives?'

'And what makes you an expert? You don't seem to have made that much of a success of running your life, so what makes you imagine that you can help run mine?'

'Maybe I can't. But I mean to try to sort this out once and for all!' She stood up, unable to sit a moment longer when her whole life was hanging in the balance. 'Maggie told me that you always ask about me when you phone her.'

'Did she?' He moved from the window and poured himself a drink, then set it down on the tray untouched.

'Yes, she did. In fact, she said that for someone who is supposedly not interested you show a great tendency to keep on asking questions.'

'Sounds as if Maggie told you a whole lot more than she should have.' He picked up the glass and downed the whisky in one go. 'What are you trying to say, Beth? That I have some sort of feelings left for you and that's why I keep asking about your welfare?' He shook his head, his eyes glittering with amusement. 'I hate to disillusion you, but that isn't so.'

'No?' She smiled faintly, moving across the room to stand just inches from him. 'And what if I said that I think that is a pack of lies?'

'More lies? I lied to you about why I married you, and now I'm lying about how I feel? That doesn't add up, Beth. One or the other must be the truth, yet you accuse me of both.'

'I was wrong. I'm not afraid to admit it now.'

'And what if I tell you that you weren't, that I did plan to use you as a cover to get Maggie back?'

'Then I wouldn't believe you. I still don't really know why you helped me in the first place, David, but I do know that you never intended to use me or the baby or our marriage *that* way!' She said the words and knew suddenly that they were the truth. David would never have used her like that, never have stooped to such subterfuge. Everything she knew about him as a person told her that and it was just a shame that she'd been too blind to see it before.

'Pretty sure of yourself, aren't you?' Colour rimmed his lean cheekbones, making her aware for the first time of how pale he was beneath the tan. There were lines of strain etched deeply on either side of his mouth and furrowed between his brows. Beth's fingers itched to smooth them away, but she knew she didn't have that right just yet, not until she had finally convinced him that she now understood the truth.

'Very sure. I was upset and hurt that night at what I overheard. It knocked me for six.' Pain flashed in her eyes, but determinedly she carried on. 'All along I knew there was something behind your reasons for marrying me. You'd admitted to me that it would help ease the situation between you and Matthew, but if you had only explained how then maybe I wouldn't have taken what I overheard to heart the way I did. All I could think of was that you had used me, that I'd been purely a cover.' She smiled sadly. 'It all added up, you see. Your determination to marry me, even your determination to keep on with our marriage when I lost the baby!'

'What did you expect me to do? Ask you to leave? It was my fault you lost your baby, Beth. The least I could do was make sure that you had the chance to get well before you made any decision about your future. I owed you that!'

'It was an accident, a tragic accident. It wasn't your fault or mine. Don't blame yourself.' His words cut deep into her heart. Had he asked her to stay with him out of some misplaced sense of duty because he had felt responsible for the loss of her child? Had that been the reason why he had suggested that they should make their marriage real, as a kind of compensation for her loss, a way that he could make amends?

Beth searched his face, desperately seeking something that would tell her that wasn't so, that her recent, precious hopes were justified, but there was nothing there to ease her tortured mind. She had to face the truth that Maggie had been wrong, so very wrong in her assessment of the situation. David had asked about her out of a sense of responsibility, nothing more, and nothing remotely like she wanted him to feel.

'I'm sorry, David,' she said quietly. 'I was a fool to come.'

'What do you want me to say, Beth? That I'm sorry?' His eyes were dark and troubled, strangely veiled so that they revealed little. 'You know how I feel and how I regret what happened.'

Regretted what? That he had married her, suggested that they should try to make a life together? Pride forbade that she should ask. She nodded, avoiding looking at him. 'I know that. At least we've managed to clear the air between us. I hated the thought that we were enemies, David.' She looked away, feeling her control slipping bit by bit. This was the last time she would ever come here, the last time she would stand in this room where once she had been offered hope and a chance for the future. She owed David a lot. The best way to repay him would be to leave now without embarrassing him any more.

She held her hand out, smiling bravely as she met his eyes. 'Thank you, David. For all you've done and all you tried to do. I . . . I shall never forget you or your kindness.'

He took her hand, his fingers cool against hers, filling her mind with memories. 'How will you manage, Beth? That room you're living in is no place for you.'

She drew her hand back. 'There is nothing wrong with it. It will do me for now until I can afford something better.'

'There is no need for you to just manage. I can find you somewhere. Leave it to me.' He slid back into the role of cool arrogance with such ease, taking over her life once more, but she couldn't allow that to happen now.

'No. Thank you. You don't need to worry about me. I am no longer your responsibility. I have a job and somewhere to live, so your commitment is at an end. Eventually I should be able to repay most of that money you paid me too.'

He swore roughly. 'You earned that money, Beth. It wasn't charity!'

'Maybe not, but I would prefer to repay you anyway.'

'So that you can wipe the slate clean? Fair enough, Beth. Whatever you decide I'll be happy to go along with.' He glanced pointedly at his watch and Beth took the hint and hurried towards the door. Just for a moment she paused in the doorway, her eyes lingering on his face, then turned and ran down the stairs, ran and ran until her lungs felt as though they would burst, but she couldn't run from the bitter-sweet pain of all those memories inside her head.

CHAPTER ELEVEN

THERE was a party going on in the flat upstairs.

Beth sat on the bed, hearing the thumping sound of the music pounding through the ceiling, but it felt as though it were coming from a million miles away. Nothing felt quite real any more, not even her.

With a ragged sigh, she got up and started to undress for bed, pulling a robe on over her long cotton nightgown. She had to go to work the following day and if she didn't get some rest she would be fit for nothing, although she couldn't imagine how she would sleep after what had happened.

Pain flashed through her as she remembered that confrontation with David and she bit her lip to hold it at bay. She couldn't break down now; she had to find the strength from somewhere to go on and rebuild a life that would never have David as its central point. She'd thought she had accepted the breakup of their relationship that night after Maggie's party but now she knew that somewhere deep in her mind she'd harboured a tiny, foolish, fragile dream that they could work it all out some way. Now there was no longer even that hope to cling to, only the cold realisation that this was the end. David had had his chance to tell her if he cared for her at all tonight and had not taken it. There was nothing left to add.

She didn't hear the knock at the door at first for the noisy throb of the music. When it came again, long and angry, she started nervously. Who could it be at this time of the night? Cautiously she eased the door open a crack, then gasped when she saw David standing outside.

'Well, are you going to let me in, or do I have to stand here all damned night?'

It was obvious from the harsh note in his voice that he was annoyed, and Beth hesitated, considering the wisdom of letting him into the room. 'What do you want?' she asked shortly.

'To come in there and sort this miserable mess out once and for all!' He pushed against the door, using his superior strength to open it wide enough so that he could walk into the room. He looked round, disgust crossing his face as he studied the peeling paintwork. 'My God, what a dump. Looks even worse now than it did the other day.'

'I'm sure you didn't come all this way to discuss the décor so would you mind telling me what you want?' She closed the door to lessen the heavy beat of the music that was starting to make her head ache, glaring coldly at him across the room. 'I thought we said all there was to say earlier on.'

'Do you think so? Well, that's mistake number one, my girl. We never even got started on what should have been said, but I have every intention of rectifying that now!' He reached out and caught her arms to pull her to him, his eyes glittering into her startled, disbelieving face for one long moment before he bent and took her mouth in a searing kiss.

Beth just had a chance to draw a shuddering breath, then she was lost as the magic that only David could create enfolded her.

Time after time his mouth moved over hers, seeking a response she was powerless to refuse. When she opened her mouth to let his tongue slide inside and tangle with hers in a rhythm of sweet, hot intimacy, she felt a shudder ripple through him, echoing the one which raced through her. Her heart went wild, pounding the blood along her veins, filling her with fire, with need, with the purely primitive desire to kiss him back and make him realise how she felt about him at last.

Slowly, almost reluctantly, he broke off the kiss, his lips skimming over her cheek before he cupped it gently with his hand and tilted her face so that he could look straight into her eyes. 'I love you, Beth. I should have told you that before, but I've fought against the idea for so long now that I was afraid to admit it even then.'

'You love me?' There was incredulity in the question and he smiled with a tenderness that made her ache.

'Yes. I've tried so hard to convince myself that I didn't, but tonight, after you left, I knew there was no way I could continue fooling myself any longer. I love you, Beth, more than I thought it possible to love any woman.'

'Even...' She hesitated, afraid to ask the question, but he understood at once.

'Even Maggie.' His voice was soft and deep, his eyes filled with warmth as he drew her close and held her tightly against him. 'I love you, Beth. You, no one else, and all I want is to hear if you can ever love me back.'

She laughed shakily, letting herself sink into the warm strength of his arms. 'I do love you, David. Surely you must know that?'

He laughed deeply, a very masculine triumph in the sound. 'I had an idea that you might!'

'Why, you...!' Beth drew back, her eyes glittering with a mixture of annoyance and pure joy, but he silenced her with a quick, fiercely possessive kiss that left her reeling. Taking her by the hand, he led her across to the bed and drew her down, sliding his arm around her waist to hold her close as though he couldn't bear to be apart from her.

'You love me, Beth, and I love you. That's all that matters. What's happened before will be painful to discuss, but cling to that fact and it won't hurt as much.'

Beth pressed against him, taking his hand between hers to twine her fingers around his in a trusting gesture. 'I will.'

'I have never really explained why I wanted to marry you so much and that's where the real problem lies. I don't think I fully understood it myself until tonight, after you'd left and I realised what I was losing by letting you go.

'When I saw you that first day in the restaurant I just wanted to help you. There was something heartbreakingly defenceless about the way you were sitting there with your world crumbling around you. Then I found out that you were pregnant and it felt like a repeat of the past.' He paused to stare into her face. 'Maggie and I were never lovers. I want to make sure that you believe that.'

'I do.' She ran a hand lovingly down his lean cheek, enjoying the fact that she had the right to touch him now.

He captured her hand, pressing a kiss to her palm before closing her fingers over the tingling spot where his lips had touched. 'Do too much of that and I'll never finish explaining and that would be a shame. We need to have everything clear between us, Beth.'

'I know. I'll try not to interrupt you again.'

'You disturb me just by being here, but...' He smiled ruefully, tucking her closer against him as he continued. 'Maggie and I were friends from the moment she married my brother, but Matthew could never accept that. Perhaps he half suspected how I felt about her before I really understood it myself, but there was never anything between us. Then one day Maggie was taken ill and came to my flat. I put her into my bed to rest and Matthew found her there.' His face was bleak and Beth shivered at the pain he still felt at the memory. 'Naturally, I suppose, he thought the worst, refused to listen to what we said. It ended up with them getting divorced, leaving Maggie pregnant with Matthew's child. He had no knowledge of it, of course; she refused to tell him about the baby. They were bleak days for her and I tried my hardest to help her. Learning that you were in virtually the same position seemed to reopen the past, Beth. It was as if fate was giving me a second test to see if I could help.'

'So I was really a substitute for Maggie?' She tried to keep the ache out of her voice, but knew she'd failed when he swore softly and pulled her close.

'No! You were never a substitute! You reminded me of the situation she'd been in, but that was all. You are totally different from her.'

'Are you sure?' She smoothed a hand over her hair, her eyes faintly sad. 'I sometimes feel that I am just a pale shadow of her.'

'A shadow?' He stared at her in surprise. 'You and Maggie are nothing at all alike, Beth. Oh, you both have red hair, but yours is more gold than red, soft and so pretty.' He smoothed a hand over her hair, twining the silky curls around his fingers. 'I've dreamt night after night about how you looked that morning lying in bed with your hair spread across the pillows like spun gold. It's made me ache on more than one sleepless night, I can tell you.'

The throbbing note of desire in his voice made her tremble and she lifted her face, wanting him to kiss her, but he barely brushed her lips with his in a fleeting caress which was more temptation than satisfaction. 'If I start kissing you now then I won't be able to stop, Beth, and we have to talk this through.'

Beth sighed, snuggling against him deliberately, smiling as she felt the immediate tension in his body. 'Anyone ever tell you that you're no fun, David Kane?'

'Frequently, but I'll have to put up with it for now. Later is when I shall try my hardest to disprove it.'

It was her turn to shudder then, her turn to feel the hot, tight spiral of desire, and she saw him smile as he acknowledged it. 'I wanted to help you, Beth, not because you were a reminder of what had gone on, but because you so very obviously needed it. Later, when I asked you to marry me, I told myself that it was because I finally wanted to end the feud with Matthew, wanted to have a home and family of my own, but it was all lies. I was falling in love with you even then, but I was afraid to face up to it when you obviously wouldn't have wanted to hear that. Not only were you pregnant, Beth, but you were still in love with the baby's father.'

'No, that's not true. I stopped loving Andrew way before then. It took me a long time to realise it, but in the end I knew it was so. But I still don't understand how marrying me could help heal the rift between you and Matthew.'

'Because it would remove the last fear from his mind. I was almost sure that he believed that there had been nothing between Maggie and me, but if I had a wife and eventually a child then he would be convinced. I wanted to wipe the slate clean, then start again and build a fresh life with you, if you were agreeable. But then the baby died.' He broke off, his face filled with sadness, then continued slowly. 'After that happened I told myself that you still needed me to help you, but it was just an excuse so that I didn't have to let you go!'

Beth smiled gently, curling her fingers into his. 'I did wonder that day you saw me in the hospital. There was an expression on your face that...' She broke off and blushed.

He touched her cheek gently. 'I was falling in love with you, Beth, and fighting it every inch of the way, terrified of making a fool of myself. But I want you to understand that I never once intended to use you or our marriage as some sort of a cover-up. Frankly, by that stage I was well and truly over Maggie!'

Her eyes shone with joy and she kissed him quickly on the corner of the mouth. 'I know that now. I've had time to think it all through and I realise that you would never do such a thing. You aren't the sort of a man to do something so underhand.'

'I'm no saint, Beth. Don't try to build me into something I'm not.'

'Maybe not, but neither are you a sinner. It might be an unfashionable description in today's world, but you are an honourable man, David, and I love you all the more because of it.'

'Do you? Are you sure that you really love me?' His eyes darkened with uncertainty for a moment, so unlike his usual arrogant assurance that her heart melted.

'Quite sure. I've been in love with you for a long time now, but, like you, was fighting the idea because I was afraid of getting hurt again.' She leant forwards, letting herself rest against him as she skimmed a line of kisses down his cheek then let her lips rest tantalisingly at the very corner of his. 'Want me to show you how much I love you, David Kane?'

'What an offer!' He started to draw her to him, intent written all over his face, then grimaced as the music pounding through the ceiling increased by a few decibels. 'What an unholy racket! There's no way that I intend to take you up on that offer to the accompaniment of that!' He stood up and pulled her to her feet, kissing her hard. 'Let's get out of here.'

'Out? Where?' Dazed by the kiss, which had left her aching for more, Beth held back as he tried to lead her to the door.

'Back home...our home, that is.' He slid his hand slowly up the length of her arm under the loose sleeve of the robe. 'I want you in my bed, Beth, your body under mine while I stroke every delectable inch of your beautiful flesh, trace every delicious curve. I want to make you mine in every way that implies, and I'll be damned if I intend to do it to the accompaniment of a heavy-metal band!'

Beth laughed, seeing the tension in his face, the need he couldn't hide, which only mirrored hers. She wanted that too, so much, but it was delicious to savour the moment when they would make love for the first time by delaying it just a while longer. 'But I'm not dressed to go out, David. You'll have to give me a few minutes to put something on.'

His eyes swept over her in open appreciation and she felt herself tingle at the warmth of the look. 'From where I'm standing you look overdressed for what I have in mind!' He let his hands slip down to hers, linking his fingers gently with hers. 'You aren't afraid, are you, Beth?'

She shook her head, her eyes brimming with love at his consideration. 'I could never be afraid of you. I love you too much. I was just teasing you, David. I...I want to make love with you just as much.'

Desire flashed hotly in his eyes and he pulled her closer, letting her feel the need in him to make her his. 'My God, Beth, you don't know how I've longed to hear you say that! I want to take care of you, cherish you, have you with me for all time.' He stared into her face. 'I want to give you a child to help make up for the one you lost.'

She smiled tenderly at him, loving him more than ever for letting her see how vulnerable he was. 'I want all that too. So much. But do you want to know one thing I want most of all?'

'What?' His lips feathered a kiss against her temples, stirring the soft curls and making her shiver with sweet anticipation.

'To hear you promise that you will always love me.'

'That is the easiest thing in the world to do.' He drew back slightly, his face very grave. 'I, David, promise that I shall always love you, Beth. How does that sound?'

'Marvellous,' she murmured, lifting her mouth up to his. 'Absolutely marvellous.'